Praise for The Last of Its Kind

"At the heart of this beautiful, delicate, and ultimately tragic novel is the relationship between a man and a large flightless bird that seems absolutely real. Sibylle Grimbert has done something quite miraculous."
—Cary Fagan, author of *A Fast Horse Never Brings Good News*

"*The Last of Its Kind* is beyond beautiful—it's essential. What joy, what blessed relief to revel in the love at its core, to see through difference and look a fellow creature in the eye."
—Alissa York, author of *Far Cry*

THE LAST OF ITS KIND

SIBYLLE GRIMBERT

Translated from the French by Aleshia Jensen

LITERATURE IN TRANSLATION SERIES
BOOK*HUG PRESS
TORONTO 2025

FIRST ENGLISH EDITION

This translation was made possible with funding from the Embassy of France in Canada and the Centre national du livre in France. Book*hug Press is grateful for their generous support.

Library and Archives Canada Cataloguing in Publication

Title: The last of its kind / Sibylle Grimbert ; translated by Aleshia Jensen.
Other titles: Dernier des siens. English
Names: Grimbert, Sibylle, author | Jensen, Aleshia, translator
Series: Literature in translation series.
Description: First English edition. | Series statement: Literature in translation series | Translation of: Le dernier des siens.
Identifiers: Canadiana (print) 20250206064 | Canadiana (ebook) 20250206072
ISBN 9781771669559 (softcover)
ISBN 9781771669580 (EPUB)
Subjects: LCGFT: Ecofiction. | LCGFT: Novels.
Classification: LCC PQ2707.R56 D4713 2025 | DDC 843/.92—dc23

Funded by the Government of Canada | Financé par le gouvernement du Canada | Canada

Book*hug Press acknowledges that the land on which we operate is the traditional territory of many nations, including the Mississaugas of the Credit, the Anishnabeg, the Chippewa, the Haudenosaunee, and the Wendat peoples. We recognize the enduring presence of many diverse First Nations, Inuit, and Métis peoples, and are grateful for the opportunity to meet and work on this territory.

To Béatrice, Michel, David, and Florent

I

FROM A DISTANCE, ONLY THE PATCH OF WHITE ON THEIR bellies stood out against the rock face, then a glinting beak, hooked like that of a bird of prey but much longer. They moved forward wobbling to the right and left, almost as though they were taking their time, testing every step for solidity, and with every step recentring their gravity with a pelvic tilt. The men, too, struggled as they approached, searching for purchase on the small island's soaked, heavy ground, backs nearly perpendicular to the beach, arms and legs spread wide like giant crabs in a row, facing the penguins that kept edging toward the shore with a precautious manner much unsuited to the situation.

It was fair weather on Eldey, the isle of sheer rock from which, in the distance, the coasts of Iceland can be seen, at least today better than most days, when there were enormous waves, though even without rain something damp and cold always stagnates in the air and clouds the view. Today the sky was a uniform grey, and you could see, in the still light, the crisp silhouettes of humans and animals as they approached each other on the shore, and then, suddenly, the men tackling the seabirds, some clubbing them, others crushing them under their weight, wringing their necks as the birds fought to break free. When the murderers rose again, they took the limp bodies with them, clutching the heads in their fists, tossing the corpses in a heap, and you could still make out the two white spots between the beak and the eye, like butterflies resting on a carcass.

The scene was short-lived, a few minutes at most. As

always when something unusual happens, the birds that could fly, those whose wings had not been stunted by centuries of happiness and tranquility, circled the cliff calling out. The ground seemed to soak up the blood—from afar no red stains could be seen—but the eggs the men had carelessly crushed on the volcanic black scree of the beach left a gleaming and certainly slippery residue. More often the men gathered the eggs and set them down, unbroken, near the pile of remains of those who had been, and would have been, their parents.

The longer you looked at the scene from the fishing boat or second rowboat waiting halfway out, the more the movements grew abstract: dots of various sizes followed repetitive geometric lines under the gauzy curtain of grey light. And you forgot that these were living things, men and great auks. The scene was no longer hypnotic, just a touch dull. Then the eye refocused on some detail: a leg, a beak, a seabird being dragged to the boat like the corpse of a child. And the faces of the mariners came back to mind, the pulse that no one had ever before felt of an animal no one had ever before touched vibrated in its chest before ceasing, palpitated under its elastic skin between the thumb and index of a hand holding the railing of the rowboat or fishing vessel.

Then, again, a sudden calm. Even the men on the island grew quiet. Something to the left disrupted what appeared to be a brief pause in the work: crumbling rock, a chunk of the cliff tumbling down. A cry came and was quickly stifled. A mariner approached the rock face, lifted a large stone, leaned down, and jumped back as he dropped it again. A beak had near bitten him. The man picked up the stone again, raised it over his head, and you could hear a kind of dense swoosh as he threw it onto the bird. Later, on the boat, he would recount how the seabird had remained still and stared at him in that moment, making no attempt to escape, its curved beak resting on the egg it was incubating. The man leaned over and picked up the dead bird and still-intact egg, which the animal's body had shielded.

Now not a single animal was left alive on Eldey. True, it had been a small colony, less than thirty or so of the creatures; some of the mariners, who had been the year before, told that it was even smaller than before. The men returned to the rowboat with the corpses. You could hear them singing. There'd be a solid supper that night of tender bird meat, an enormous protein-filled omelette to wolf down.

As the rowboat from whence Auguste had observed the scene headed back to the vessel, he saw a black shape in the water near the boat. It looked a little like the mop Mrs. Bridge used to wash the floors. He bent over, grabbed the bird, and felt its panic, its strength, compromised as it was—or else it would have swum away—and when he pulled it onto the boat, the creature, with a stumpy broken wing hung at its belly, let out a cry. It tried to bite Gus, its one good wing stretched out as straight as possible, its body, the height of Gus's waist, slid between his hands, solid as muscle. But like the rest of its kind, it was helpless out of water. Someone grabbed a net from the bottom of the boat and threw it onto the bird, and it found itself trapped, struggling in vain, emitting repeated squawks that, according to one of the men, sounded like the cries of a witch.

On the boat they put the great auk in a cage. It stopped crying once inside. They brought over a fish, but the auk refused it. From behind the bars, it stared at Gus, furious or hateful even, and Gus's hand shook as he dropped another fish at its feet. Until that second he hadn't noticed the penguin-like creature's expression. He imagined himself telling the naturalist who had employed him that a great auk was capable of an accusatory stare. In truth, Auguste had never believed he would have the chance to capture one. He had rather pictured sending a dead specimen to Lille, to be stuffed. He'd gotten on the fishing boat expressly because the mariners were passing the island of Eldey, the nesting spot of the last-known great auk colony of the region. But it had never occurred to him to bring back a living creature, an animal he could then study in depth before it died, wretchedly, in captivity, as likely it would.

Later the bird slept, or pretended to. Gus watched it closely through the bars. He noted that, while he had always known a great auk to be feathered, its down was surprising; until then he had imagined the great auk to be an oily creature, akin to a seal. At dinner, swallowing a bite of auk meat, he felt that a seal must taste similar too. The meat was nauseating and fatty. He didn't take a second helping.

The journey back to the Orkney Islands took nearly two days. The auk kept its head turned toward the railing when it paced past them, to the point that neither Gus, who took an interest, nor the sailors, who didn't, could see anything but the bird's back and its motionless tail, its neck stooped so low that it appeared headless. No one questioned whether the cage was too narrow, except for one fisherman who suggested they fasten a cord to one leg and let it out on the water, but Gus refused, fearing the bird would break free. Luckily the sea spray, the humid sea air, and the rain kept the creature drenched.

Back in Stromness, the largest town in the Orkneys, where he'd settled six months earlier in January of 1834 to study the fauna, Gus found a slightly larger cage than the one on the ship, which he placed, with the bird shut inside, in a room of the house he was renting. Mrs. Bridge, who cooked his meals and cleaned the house, was scandalized by the presence of this ghastly, terrifying beast that had no business being indoors. Gus had to promise that she would never be asked to go near it. After two days he moved the cage to a fairly large room on the main floor—where he decided he would work from then on, far from her mop and bucket—and instructed the old woman never to enter.

Every day Gus poured pitchers of water over the cage. The bird would spread its wings, crane its neck, pass its beak across its belly then across its back for minutes at a time. It was the only time it moved, except, of course, to swallow the fish Gus left at its feet. The auk would hop back feebly, then lower its beak between its closed feet and snap it up. The rest of the time it stood perfectly still, beak nestled in its chest, body slumped over as though its feet were lashed down. When the bird stood in profile, Gus could sometimes see its black or very deep brown eye staring out at him, strikingly hostile. Gus felt almost afraid. He told himself Mrs. Bridge must be right, the creature must be dangerous; the seaman had said as much, after all: It looks like a witch, with its hooked beak and hoarse cry.

That beak was a true wonder. Gus had already remarked on the single engraving of a great auk he had seen in *Buffon's Natural History*, an engraving based on a description and not, as he would be the first to do, observed in nature—at that thought alone, he flushed hot and his heart began to race. Up close the beak proved more bizarre than anything he could have imagined. Nothing like a parrot's beak, for instance. It was longer, closer—in terms of drawing it, that is—to a crab's pincer in the space where a nose would be. It was black, of course, shiny too, but with thick stripes across it, neither pretty nor ugly, as impressive as the markings painted on faces in villages in Africa or near Australia.

THERE WAS NO IGNORING IT: THE AUK WAS WITHERING away in its cage. Three days had sufficed for an odour of rot to invade the room. When Mrs. Bridge passed the study door to clean the second floor, her aged, austere face crumpled and puckered into a sort of cone, as though she were trying to clench her mouth and all other orifices as tightly as humanly possible. For the last two days, she had also worn a crocheted bonnet that covered her ears, no doubt to afford further protection from miasmas. She avoided looking at Gus, who was left thinking he must be the source of the stench. Perhaps being shut in the study with his bird had, in the end, impregnated him with an odour of rotting fish mixed with thick-laden dust.

He had to be quick. So quick that he did not stop to write Garnier, a naturalist at Lille's Museum of Natural History and his employer, to notify him of the sensational capture of such a rare specimen. What he had to do was sketch the auk before it died, from every possible angle. Of course, facing a bird stuck in its cage, he was forced to demonstrate some creativity. The first few days, every time Gus had poured buckets of water over its head, the auk had regained some air of normality. But now nothing worked. It remained still, nearly cowering when the water touched it, since to reproduce the moments when the auk incarnated the very essence of its species, Gus had been flooding the cage, fetching bucket after bucket. He knew it was idiotic, but who exactly until this moment had drawn a bird twisting its neck behind its back to clean itself?

Gus was a good sailor, an adventurous type. And now, as the very first man to observe a living great auk at his leisure, and also a singular traveller, he was potentially a valuable assistant to the Museum of Natural History, which would be sure to finance his subsequent voyages. Though his zoological background was somewhat thin, having, in fact, studied pharmacy, he knew enough to see that this bird, sometimes compared to an African penguin, but of an altogether different species (it lived in the North Atlantic after all), had become a legendary animal since its disappearance from the coasts of North America, where hundreds of thousands of them had once lived.

Meanwhile the creature seemed to be festering on its feet, and it was dire. It was shedding and looked a complete mess, and less and less like how one would expect a great auk to appear: sleek, imposing, skin with the sheen of a top hat. Entire sheets of plumage whirled around the room, its body had become a sort of world map where continents of down adjoined the oceanic surface, glossy with feathers, the whole in a chaos devoid of logic just like the earth itself. It took Gus two days to realize his auk was moulting. What rotten luck. The bird moped about in its cage, displaying little to enjoy in the way of a pleasant attitude, neither grooming its feathers nor swallowing the fish tossed its way. To be precise, it was no more than a shapeless creature, the rough resemblance of a bird who would be a poor model for any sketch.

On the fourth day, it refused to eat.

What an obstinate beast, thought Gus. No intelligence, no foresight. A stupid animal, in fact, that would rather die of hunger than remain caged. How exasperating. Would a man stop eating just because he'd been imprisoned? No, the auk was clearly weak-willed in the face of adversity—a defeatist. It stuck its head into its breast, evoking a stick of wood, some sacred Druidic object, or a menhir from Stonehenge in miniature.

Each day at the sight of the auk, Gus was struck by its size, as though he had to get used to it all over. He would observe the bird, but there was nothing new to study. If it refused to move, he would never know how it positioned its feet on the ground, how it held its neck while walking, nor would he be able to accurately describe its cry. All of that he'd have to invent. He had an animal no one had ever been as close to, and he'd be forced to doctor the observations. He still had to write to Garnier, bring him up to date, ask what he should do with the fowl. He'd have to do so before the bird's death, otherwise Garnier might not believe him, or might be angry he hadn't written sooner. He might even reproach Gus for the manner in which he'd cared for the animal in his charge. Yes, he needed to write today, omitting mention of the deplorable state of the great auk, or perhaps hedging his description so as not to arouse excessive optimism in Garnier.

He opened the cage. In such a miserable state, the bird would not escape. He returned to his desk, leaving the auk to its own devices. Nothing happened. It stayed where it was. Gus went back over to it, held a finger out near its wing and poked into its sickly feathers, as one would touch a troubling unknown substance, then jerked his finger back. He had felt the coarse, delicate, and bony texture of the wing. Then he remembered the animal had been wounded on Eldey. Yet it did not seem to be suffering, since it had not even flinched.

Gus made a cooing sound as though calling a pigeon. The auk kept its head stuck into its breast, dull and motionless, "empty" thought Gus—an empty, listless thing. Then he tired of observing it and returned to his desk.

A sound made him look up from the letter he was writing to Garnier. The auk, a dozen centimetres from the cage, had just fallen. It was shaking on the ground in stationary distress, as though trying to swim across the terracotta tiles. Gus went over to it; as soon as his foot was near the bird, it moved its beak to bite the ankle just within reach, above the Achilles tendon. Gus stepped back, whispering "gently now," as though addressing a puppy. It emitted several highly unpleasant and hoarse, shrill sounds that would be sure to throw Mrs. Bridge into a panic. It writhed around on the floor, slid from right to left, without moving forward even a millimetre; its injured wing sometimes fell under the weight of its body, which only increased its cries, as the bottoms of its feet floundered and its claw scraped the ground.

Gus had the idea to grab the animal from behind. And it wasn't a bad one: It scared the bird to the point where it quieted and, between Gus's hands, went almost limp and motionless once more. No doubt the bird expected to die, resigned before an incomprehensible destiny that had extracted it from its aquatic environment and prevented it from perceiving the dangers to its life. Gus felt its heart beating beneath the downy newly formed feathers covering skin softer than he could ever imagine, something that seemed also velvety, as smooth as kid gloves, yet thrumming, quick as a locomotive. "Easy now," he said again, and he placed the auk upright. It was wobbly. The muscles in its feet are swollen from days in captivity, thought Gus. After putting it back in its cage, Gus brought over a fish and left the cage door open.

He could no longer focus on the letter. Back at his desk, he could only watch the bird. He couldn't help it; he would try to finish a sentence, but he would look up, and the sentence never reached an end, nor did the mental draft that should have preceded it. He heard Mrs. Bridge go from room to room banging doors behind her, dragging the furniture, beating the rugs to show her offence at being forced to share air with a wild beast, and a noisy one at that. She was afraid, and the auk was afraid, yet Gus was calm.

He gave up on the letter. Time passed, but he didn't notice. The bird moved its neck, rubbed its beak against the floor. It would swallow, then freeze. It cried out, then quieted. Gus stayed where he was, leaning his head right and left, following the animal's movements as he leaned his chest flat against the table to observe it more closely without disturbing it. The front door of the house slammed shut. This time Gus stood up and left the study, only to find Mrs. Bridge's apron hanging from the front door handle, like a flag some enemy plants in your yard as a declaration of war. From the window, Gus saw the old woman come through the entryway waving her arms. With strips of lace streaming from her bonnet, she looked like a scarecrow in a raging storm.

Gus went back to his study. He did not have time to chase after Mrs. Bridge; he could not leave the auk. In truth there was no question: The moment he had laid eyes on the animal again, he had fallen captive to even the slightest of movements, which were similar to what he had already observed, except that any variation in the light or a varying emphasis of the beak on its feathers changed everything. Time passed, still without him noticing. Finally the bird left its cage and took two steps, and then a third, balancing to one side and the other, its healthy wing spread away from its breast. Without thinking, Gus grabbed a fish and drew nearer, knelt down a few feet away and placed the fish on the ground. The auk paused, edged closer, paused again, then took another step.

On the white wall, the outline of the bird's beak stood out in sharp relief. Its profile was visible as it turned to look at Gus and stared at him with only its right eye, its body still facing more or less forward. Gus looked at the iris, a light brown, or at least lighter than the pupil. He was surprised;

he had been expecting a solid colour, deeper browns. A milky circle bordered the iris and diluted into a sliver of white, more troubling still. In the bird's eye he could discern intelligence and, of course, mistrust, but from somewhere deep down, as though the animal were thinking, figuring out what to make of this unknown creature before it. It was also standing its ground, which showed a certain amount of courage. Gus carefully observed the one-eyed gaze of a creature ruled by pure instinct. He had the impression of finding himself face to face with a thoughtful, courageous animal, one that appeared to calculate the danger and the unknown that he, Gus, represented. All of this because of a somewhat pale iris, which so resembled those he had seen in the eyes of friends, without ever thinking much of it.

Maybe solitude was starting to weigh on him and a single eye seemed extraordinary only because it was alive and able to stare back and see, see *him*. Just then, he noticed the patches of white feathers the auk had above its beak had disappeared. This was a shock. It was no longer a question of a gaze, of depth, of creatures seeing and sizing up one another, but a question of an animal that had changed, that was moulting, but also one that had lost a fundamental defining feature. Gus returned to his desk to jot down the detail in his notebook, but as he did, he decided that, upon further reflection, he would continue to draw the auk with its highly recognizable spots: the clean shapes near the sharp, clear irises encircling narrowed pupils.

It was already five in the afternoon, and not yet dark. The bird kept moving, mostly along the back wall of the room. When it came face to face with an object, such as a piece of furniture—the chest of drawers or a chair—it would sometimes tap the thing with its beak, as though to figure out its material of origin. By half past five, it had made its way across the width of the room, around six metres. Ten minutes later came a knock at the door. Through the window Gus saw Mr. Buchanan, the Stromness notary. The bird would have to be put back in its cage. Gus lunged forward and grabbed the auk from behind, picking it up as though it were a duck. Everything happened so quickly; it seemed the bird had no time to dodge him. It let out a low but furious sound, a croak of resignation and offence, as its clawed feet batted against Gus's stomach.

As Buchanan delivered a second volley of cheerfully polite taps on the door, Gus shouted, "I'm coming!" the bird still in his arms, one of which was around its wings and the other at the base of its neck. He held its tense torso as it struggled weakly against him, with the same fatalistic intensity of its cry. It was another story, however, at the door of the cage. Gus did not know how to fold the auk to fit it inside, and quickly. The bird had gone completely limp, either out of fear or strategically, to avoid an accident that would damage it, so much so that it was difficult, in this rag-doll state, to push it through the cage door. "I'm coming!" Gus shouted again to Buchanan, his frustration growing and his forehead dampening. He shoved the animal's head through first, then pushed on its back end, which swayed slightly in protest. The auk was still in this pathetic position when, after closing one door, Gus headed to another.

SEATED IN THE MAIN ROOM OF RATHER SMALL SIZE, neither man was drinking. Both were nearly the same age, a fact Gus found galling. Clearly a scandalized Mrs. Bridge had called in Buchanan, after she'd been forced to fight off a creature with an eagle's beak, a soup tureen for a body and wings for handles, feet like a duck's—some sort of flightless birdlike beast with an apparent ill temper. To her, it may as well have been a platypus, whose existence she had never, in all her life, imagined.

"Try to appease her, show her a token of respect," offered Buchanan, as though his advanced age of twenty-four qualified him to give advice to a man of twenty-three. "Old women around these parts are remarkably good at being a nuisance, but they're also quick to surrender. You'll see."

They sank into their armchairs facing the cold fireplace. Buchanan rolled a cigarette, thus occupying his thin white fingers, his face a coordinated pink, yet also thin and white, leaning over the rolling papers. Gus wondered if Buchanan had come to give him some lesson on the best way to deal with the inhabitants of this secluded island enclosed in fog as though suspended above the rest of the world; however, he could tell already that Buchanan's slow motions were intended to buy time, and favour, before he came to the real reason for his visit. Gus would have done the same, but for the moment he was thinking of the animal shut in its cage, ruffled, or at least creased. He wasn't going to hide it: He did not believe himself to be committing any moral infraction by keeping a singular seabird specimen in this lost, backward town. He did not believe Mrs. Bridge had any grounds for feeling hurt or slighted. But neither did he wish to cede to the curiosity of this distinguished man, who was also clearly anemic, no doubt due to decades of curtains of rain obstructing the sun.

In truth, Gus was growing impatient. After fifteen minutes he rose from his chair, a sign known around the world as the end of a meeting. But Buchanan did not budge. He only went from translucent to deep pink, his entire face tainted with the colour of his cheeks. A silence followed, causing Gus to feel he should sit down again, and to wonder if the young man were not about to have a stroke. But no, once seated on the chair cushions, the Scotsman regained his pallor—which for him signified good health—and smiled.

"I'd like to see the bird," he said outright.

Gus was caught off guard, or, if he was honest with himself, he found himself jealous. He had never tried to conceal the auk from Mrs. Bridge, though where had that gotten him? But showing the bird to someone his own age—someone smart and kind, a man who could have been a friend, should he one day entertain the absurd idea of settling in the Orkneys for good—seemed out of the question.

"It would disturb it too much," came his short, polite response with a certain logical merit. "Perhaps some other time. I have to try my best to keep it alive. The bird is my responsibility. If I can send it to the Natural History Museum, that would be best."

To show that the topic was now closed, Gus crossed his legs and leaned back in the armchair, set to engage in an hour or two of general conversation to wear out his guest until he gave up and left. Just the thought of Buchanan standing before the auk horrified him. Who knows, perhaps Buchanan would know how to approach it, perhaps he understood the animal better than Gus, perhaps his knowledge of great auks was far vaster.

"You know about the market?"

Gus was sure Buchanan had uttered such a mysterious question to foreclose any noncommittal answer. He settled for a cold reply that he hoped would convey his disinterest in this market and the fact he had no idea what it was.

"The market where they sell skins, or bits of auks and other birds: feathers, beaks, eggs. They're worth a great deal. You have a fortune on your hands, even if it doesn't seem like there will be any eggs."

Gus was still unsure what Buchanan was driving at, other than that he apparently wanted to buy the auk to sell its feathers somewhere, although Gus didn't see anything particularly special about them, nothing, for instance, as striking as those of an ostrich. But he had to admit he really wasn't all that knowledgeable when it came to trinkets, baubles, and sundries.

"How many auks were on Eldey when you went?" asked Buchanan.

"After the men left, about thirty."

"Oh." Buchanan said no more.

Gus was stunned. Buchanan, in his chair in the sitting room / library / dining area, had said "Oh" in surprise and then gone quiet, as though Gus were a child or too ignorant to waste time explaining what seemed so clear. This time it was Gus who turned red, but his complexion was more forgiving than his guest's. He cleared his throat and, as he'd done before, stood to indicate to the Orcadian the end of this delightful visit.

Buchanan looked at Gus standing before him, and this time his complexion remained pallid. His eyes were such a light brown that they bordered on the khaki-green hue of certain muds. His smile widened until it became a subtle line at the bottom of his excessively narrow face. Gus had no choice but to sit down. His vigour and strength now seemed graceless and coarse compared with the patience of the elegant man next to him. The great auk colonies were dwindling, he had learned from someone shocked to find Gus so unaware.

"I wonder where they're going. At the turn of the century, there were still many of them near Newfoundland, before they migrated here, and now numbers seem to be diminishing here as well. People sell parts of them as trophies," continued Buchanan. "The whole world wants some part of the great auk. And its rareness only makes it more valuable, of course."

Gus listened, unable to hide his surprise as he might have liked; yet he had no reason to feel hurt for not knowing something in an area in which he had never claimed expertise and had fallen into by chance alone. Then, he asked himself whether Buchanan's words might not contain the suggestion that he, Gus, was perhaps using science as a mere pretext for profit. But no, that wasn't it. Buchanan was simply warning him of the dangers of housing the great auk under his roof, in the heart of a village of seafarers all too aware of its worth.

"And now, may I see it?" asked Buchanan.

Gus hesitated, then agreed.

The afternoon light in the study had dimmed. When Gus went to light at least a candle on his desk, Buchanan motioned for him to stop. In the dusk, they could make out the cage and a mass like a blob of butter, but black, and perhaps the silver of the bird's beak, though Gus figured this must be a trick of the light. Buchanan kept still, speechless before the somewhat anodyne sight so far. They heard its feet moving across the cage's metal floor, and Buchanan took a step forward and bent down for what seemed to Gus, still at the door, to be a very long few minutes.

Buchanan silently watched the quiet animal, which seemed asleep. From the door, Gus saw two abstract shapes that he had trouble making out, other than the detail of Buchanan's light-coloured shirt collar floating like a ghost embryo, signalling the location of his neck, head, and, down a little farther, his back. He stuck an arm out to the side and waved it, to tell Gus to light the candle. And Gus obliged, feeling that he was participating in some sort of ritual: stepping quietly across the floor, striking a match as quietly as he could. The act felt sacred, or at least gravely serious, and his throat tightened, though he did not know why.

Yellow light spilled into the room, dimming as it reached Buchanan and the auk. Gus approached, slowly still so as not to frighten the two of them observing each other. He knelt down next to Buchanan. He could see that Buchanan had locked eyes with the bird; and they were looking at one another quite intently, concentrated but mostly calm. For the first time, Gus saw the auk at peace.

He felt as though he had entered Buchanan's perspective, seeing what the other saw: an incredible, immense creature, accentuated by dusk and solitude. Gus's eyes adjusted to the dim orange light. Details emerged out of the darkness. Before he had only recorded them, but now he looked carefully at an old, dishevelled feather poised to fall out, and an entire patch of almost shining new feathers ready to come forth and flourish on the animal's breast, on which he noticed two slight bulges where its heart must be, between them a small dip, throbbing and alive.

"Look at that. I've only ever seen dead ones," said Buchanan.

"You should go out on one of the boats one day."

"I don't care for sailing. And you said there were no more than thirty left on Eldey. After you left, if I understood right, I doubt those numbers improved."

Gus didn't answer. He was neither angry nor upset, nor did he feel guilty, he simply looked at the auk. Speaking, any effort to project his voice, would have distracted him. He wondered why he had been insensitive to the auk's beauty and majesty up to now. It must have been the effect of the late afternoon, the drizzle outside, the reverence Buchanan lent to the scene.

Gus reached forward to open the cage door. The auk, as though trustful now, carefully came out, still wobbly on its feet. It will never be comfortable out of water, thought Gus. The auk looked funny when it walked, a fact Gus had missed before. But perhaps the creature's demeanour had been less natural, perhaps the fervour with which Buchanan was observing it felt reassuring.

What Gus saw was a unique penguin-like creature, an animal unlike any he had seen before, one he struggled even to see as a bird. For him, in that moment, it was more like a fish breathing out of water, or a goose that could swim, a chimera with feathers for scales, weak wings, and the beak of a bird of prey, which was, no doubt, useless as well. At the end of the day, an anomaly, and a disproportionate mould of the many of the penguins he had seen on his travels, or the small razorbills that could dive and fly, just as common as seagulls.

Buchanan took a pitcher of water and went to pour it over the bird. It smoothed its plumage, as Gus had seen the bird do before, and slid its beak under its wing along its back. Gus thought: Just like the rest of its kind, it is doing what it must to survive; it wants to survive. Then watching its adept movements—the beak searching for old feathers again, smoothing the new ones, distinguishing one from the other, pausing at one spot and shaking its head nervously as though scratching irritated skin just there—Gus no longer saw a specimen of the great auk but rather one animal in particular: *this* one, the one he had saved. He watched the age-old gestures, habits learned, and teachings passed on, an intelligence manifested in this exact creature. He saw the auk he knew, the one he had fed and touched with his own hand. This creature, he told himself, must have reactions, needs and wants, this creature was at once unique and an exemplar of an entire species.

He and Buchanan left the room together, as though this curious yet uneventful experience had a stifling effect. They had watched the sea fowl groom itself; it could have been for hours or two minutes, or even years. It was at once an ordinary act and one of untold value, for all the birds and for that one in particular, and from that moment on they would be aware of the subtlest changes in repetitive movement, the slightest nuance in the beak's trajectory; the almost imperceptible oscillation of a wing would be felt as an irrevocable commotion.

The two men were back in the armchairs. They poured themselves a whisky this time, to decant the excitement and emotion. They heard the wind outside again, and the waves on the shore. Buchanan stared at the liquid in his glass, as though he had spied a tiny auk swimming inside.

"Auguste, it didn't enrage you to see those men massacre the colony?"

His deep voice carried accusatory undertones. Enrage him? Why would it? Men ate beasts, beasts ate other beasts: That was the law of the world. And yet there was something disturbing about it. There was the memory of panic, the pleasure the men took in the act, how brutal the slaughter had been, the sight of a great auk protecting its egg, then seeing that egg crushed under a rock. It was true. Gus had not posed questions. He had watched everything as though in a dream. Or perhaps not. Perhaps he had stared at the ground, or watched from the corner of his eye, glancing up from the wood planks of the rowboat to the beach, then back down again.

Buchanan kept looking at his glass, as though contemplating Gus in all his shame or weakness was too painful—Gus, a pharmacist and a biologist completely free of scruples, unable to see ugliness, violence, or human passion, only progress, or pure science, or his own interests, those of a frustrated adventurer.

Thanks to the candles and the light of the fire, the room was lighter than the study where the auk was kept. It brought Gus back to civilization, to honest men settled into the cushions of their chairs after the day's labours, far from wild animals and brutal mariners. Except it was dark out, the wind was whipping the house, and the eddies of the waves isolated them, he and Buchanan, as though they were inside a shipwreck. He longed to be in a tavern amid the shouts of drinkers, the wild laughter over trivial things, the songs belting out along ribbons of boozy breath. Gus wanted a pint, not a syrupy whisky, a beer with foam like the down of a moulting auk.

Why was he thinking about the bird again? Why did the thought of something white and airy conjure the image of that sea fowl tousled in decaying feathers? Was having a wild animal in his home really so extraordinary? In Africa, kings kept lions, it was said. Did they wake up each morning marvelling at the fauna at their feet? Or did their wonder dissipate at some point? He was just like Buchanan, for whom all paths led back to the bird.

"You're going to have to be very careful," said Buchanan.

Gus felt the words were a threat. But no, Buchanan was looking at him now, he had put down the glass, which no longer contained the image of a bird of any kind. Half his face was orange in the firelight, the other half was in the dark—grey but a pale shade thereof, as though immune to the full effect of the shadows. They smiled at one another. The wind was blowing, the ocean rolling, and they had returned to that room, to a house near the shoreline where a rational explanation existed for all these noises, as did a logical and scientific explanation for the presence of a living great auk specimen.

"Hungry?" he asked Buchanan, for the sake of saying something and breaking the tension in the room.

But Buchanan ignored him. "They'll try to sell everything, right up to a broken bit of claw, an eye if they knew how to preserve it. It's a huge market. Museums want specimens for their collections, vendors want to sell those specimens to them, collectors will pay a fortune for pretty tobacco boxes made from their beaks, if it's what's in fashion."

"I'm not going to sell the great auk. I'm sending it to Lille—alive!" Was poor Gus an ignorant child? He himself found his statement naive and the final emphasis stupid. In the darkness he could feel his face redden.

"Is that what you really think? You're a scientist. The museum paid for your trip and living expenses, so I suppose they'll also be the ones who decide what to do with the creature."

It was true. Gus had not really given thought to what Garnier might ask of him. He wanted to leave Stromness, to set out on a more prestigious expedition if he could, to lesser known countries. He had picked up the great auk as though it were a rare flower to be catalogued in Jussieu's collections.

Human morals, be they sentimental or grandiose, were of no interest to him.

Just then the wind, the waves, the cold, the night, and the loneliness resurfaced, along with the silhouette of the captive auk in the next room, and with it the inkling of danger conjured by Buchanan with his face long as a prophet's, with whom he could not for a moment imagine sharing a casual pint in the pub, or shooting jokes back and forth. This pensive man who scarcened the air in the room, and Gus's thoughts returned to life outside of those walls, even in the somewhat drab streets of Stromness, to the night, under the rain.

"Did I scare you?" Buchanan laughed, becoming once again a friend of Gus's own age, his accomplice to a thrilling discovery. The air began flowing again; something of ordinary existence came back, breaking the dramatic, excessive spell.

"I know those men," said Gus. "In a month here I've seen many of them. I went out fishing with them, twice. I've seen them. How courageous they are."

"And that means they're loyal men who'd never steal from you?"

"The bird's mine. And they're well aware. They made no objections when I captured it."

"And what's your price for it? Because you have a price. A career at the Museum of Lille? Your name as a donor on a stuffed specimen? I'm not asking because I care. I just believe you should be aware. The things we value, others can value too. You're beholden to the same people in the end..."

The alcohol was making Gus feel heavy. He needed to get up. He felt short of breath and, from time to time, for a few seconds, his eyes would close. Buchanan must be tired too. He stood up at the same time as Gus. Neither could say who opened the door first. Gus did not notice Buchanan put on his coat and hat, when already his tall silhouette was opening the garden gate, his bendy, lanky body swallowed by the darkness of the street.

After he left, Gus went back to the study. The creature was in the corner opposite the cage. It emitted little cooing sounds, short low-pitched trilling noises, as though trying to gather its strength to impress Gus with a terrifying cry. Gus went closer to it and, as he'd done before, grabbed the bird from behind, without thinking of what would come next once he had the auk in his arms.

The ocean was lightly choppy, not to excess, just what was necessary. And this was lucky, because the foam off the waves was more visible than ever in the dark. As they left, Gus had the time to grab a cord hanging by chance on the coat stand near the door.

As he walked the fifty metres separating them from the shore, the auk, stuck in Gus's arms, kept agitating then going rigid, as though exhausted by the excitement. Its feet had scratched Gus's stomach, and its claws, enthusiastic or stupefied, pierced through his vest at times and even his shirt, scraping the skin. Gus had paced onward, determined, feeling like an automaton with his mind filled and fixed on a goal of whose relevance he was, in fact, unsure.

Yet it was simple. He was possessed by one thought alone: He had to bring the great auk to the ocean. The cord could be tied to one foot, as they did on the boats. He counted on the sea fowl's stunned state to manage to attach it. Automation had the true advantage of rendering actions precise and removing hesitation, if needed, to grab the foot while kneeling on the creature as it instinctively struggled, and winding a cord tightly around it. Which is what Gus did, with undeniable success. When he finished, he was not even sure if the bird had kept silent, or if the wind and waves had drowned out the cry.

He set the bird down on the pebbly beach. He remembered the beaches in northern France where he had walked on the sand, and he felt they must be easier to walk across, but then again the auk was used to this. The bird walked slowly at first, then lay flat where the water was a few centimetres deep. Suddenly it changed, like bread dough beginning to rise. Not that it became any bigger, but seemed suddenly to prosper, to alter, to find its age-old shape, as a limp glove regains its dignity when a hand slips into it. Perhaps it was washing itself of the filthiness of solid ground, plunging its head under water, turning its body one way and the other. Gus could only see the auk's white stomach as it burst up and dove in. And then it disappeared altogether.

It took only a few seconds. Gus felt the cord tighten before he even had time to worry. The bird tugged so hard that Gus wrapped the rope right around his hand. He had not expected the auk to be so strong. He stood on the shore with the cord biting at his right hand and chafing the left when he changed hands for a moment's relief. He leaned back, unsteady because of the rocks. The bird still had not resurfaced, and in the darkness, Gus wasn't sure he could see it. A struggle began between the two, and Gus knew in the end he would lose. He needed to pull, pull with all his strength, to pull the bird quickly back to the beach. But it was doing underwater arabesques; what Gus felt most was not its strength but its agility, which would wear him out in the end as he faltered on the uneven bits of rock that were so shaky and jagged he could not even sit down, which would have been more comfortable and made it easier to grip the cord with all his weight.

He waded into the sea up to his knees. The water was

glacial, but the tension dulled the cold. He knelt, no, he sat, the water now up to his chest. The rocks felt more bearable there. Sometimes a wave crashed into his shoulders. When one pushed him in the right direction, toward the shore, it lent strength to his resistance, and he could feel the auk at the other end of the cord draw nearer. He was no longer cold, nor sore, nor able to determine how long he had been struggling against the rope. Later, when he thought back on it, he figured that all of this had lasted no more than ten minutes.

Gus was afraid of losing the auk. He had seen the bird as an enemy, showing it no more sympathy than he would a common prisoner looking to escape, and later a creature ignorant of the risks it was running, a creature he had to protect. By the end of the struggle, though, when the bird reappeared in the water near where he was sitting, he thought that, above all, it was an animal alone. He was alone, too, in that moment, awkward in an element unsuited to him, soaked, frozen, encumbered by the heavy clothes that clung to his body. The bird stayed near him, floating on the water like a common duck. What was incredible was that the bird looked happy.

He caught his breath. He couldn't see the auk well in the dark, but it was not important, because he could feel it, he thought, and the auk could feel his presence too. The situation had reversed: Gus had become the displaced one, adrift in the other's universe. He contemplated this dark, disquieting, violent world. He listened to its perpetual noise: the wind, the waves, the sea swell. And now he admired the auk, and, because he admired it, he thought that if the animal disappeared one day, it would be a sad event, like the loss of a kind of knowledge, the disappearance of a way of moving through a hostile element, something different from the seabirds flying, the seals swimming, the fish he couldn't see under the water.

Finally he got to his feet. The wind and the air seemed to seep and whip through to the marrow of his bones; he was freezing, his lips surely dry and cracked. He picked up the bird, and it resisted, but gently as a pet might, without biting, like a cat digging its claws into the carpet when you try to pick it up, but who then lets you do so nonetheless. They went home, the bird no doubt comfortable outside at night and Gus petrified, slowed by his wet clothes, exhausted upon reaching the front door. He took a few moments before drying off, to put the bird in the study—but not in the cage. Before leaving the room, he just had time to see it glide across the floor, suddenly deft and quick out of water, a sort of thin, slippery rocket that crashed into the dresser and literally flattened itself under it. Gus undressed before the fire and fell asleep under a blanket, sitting up in the armchair, as close as possible to the fire.

MRS. BRIDGE HAD COME BACK THE NEXT DAY, WITH no explanation. She had contented herself with fussing about the house, her face stern and strained, while avoiding the study. Buchanan arrived late that afternoon. Mrs. Bridge would glance over at them and whistle through her teeth, lifting her eyes to the ceiling. Once everyone had left at nightfall, Gus brought the bird out swimming.

On the fourth night, he went to the port tavern. He wanted some excitement and to see the men with whom he had gone out cod fishing on the trip where he found the great auk. As he stepped into the clammy heat, sweat began to bead on his cheeks and forehead. The brouhaha came as a shock at first. It was precisely what he had hoped for. Straightaway, he saw Armstrong sitting at a table. He sat down next to him with a beer. Armstrong had been on the boat with Gus. He must have been near forty, maybe a little less, and what remained of his teeth were yellow and black—not that Gus's were entirely intact, or an ideal shade. The fisherman's hands looked enormous and knotted, covered in intriguing scars, a paralyzed ring finger frozen in the form of a hook.

He did not ask Gus for news of the bird. What for Gus had been an extraordinary and complicated adventure was surely for Armstrong no more than a blip out at sea, neither noteworthy nor interesting. Gus dared not broach the subject. In any case, he had spoken of it often enough to Buchanan. And it was because of Buchanan that he now felt he was committing some transgression by coming to the pub, a den of debauchery rife with greed where someone would happily, he had been warned by the notary, cut your throat for a pint. But Gus knew these men. They had spent a month at sea together, after all.

The men laughed, talked of everything and nothing, pausing to listen to their fellow mariners, glad for the break. Sometimes voices rose as though in anger, then lowered again, drowned out by shouts across the room. The pub seemed to have been taken over by shoulders, hunched over tables and the bar, a stooped sea of them, pipes or pints jutting out, lowered faces swaying and hidden under hats and caps or beards, and necks curved like a turtle's.

At the bar, Einarsson, an Icelander who had been on the beach at Eldey during the slaughter, drank his beer, by turns laconic and loquacious, the heart of the conversation. Gus startled at the sight of him, so much so that he took a step back, as though the image of a man holding an auk with a slit throat had appeared between him and Einarsson leaning on the bar—the memory of his black mouth opening like a chasm at the bottom of his face, shrill squeals of joy surprising from this hulk of a man. Gus felt embarrassed for being so sensitive.

"Where's that beast of yours?" Einarsson hissed into his ear.

Gus must have been daydreaming, because he had not noticed Einarsson leave the bar and sidle up to him at the table. "Someone from France is picking it up in Edinburgh," lied Gus, instinctively. Buchanan's warnings had not gone unheard. Einarsson's hopes seemed blighted for a moment.

"We all have our work, I guess. Yours is to send the bird to the continent. Not that I see the point." Then after a pause, "If it dies before then, I'd gladly take it off your hands."

"Even dead I'll have to send it to France," said Gus.

Einarsson's disappointment returned, with a touch of

surprise, as though he sensed Gus to be not entirely sincere.

"And who says it belongs to you? You wouldn't have found it without us."

"Leave him be," Armstrong cut in, his tired eyes looking inward, not at Gus or at anyone else.

Einarsson let out a sound, maybe the start of a sentence, then swallowed it again and kept quiet, as though holding back a secret, and shot Gus a sneer of a smile instead before heading back to the bar. Uneasy and cowed a bit by Einarsson's presence, Gus remained seated across from Armstrong.

"Those birds are getting hard to find. Everyone's after them," said Armstrong.

"You killed all of them on Eldey, you could have let them live..."

"What for? They're good for eating. Puts hair on your chest. Must have tried some yourself, no?"

Gus had tried a bite, or had it been a piece of omelette? Even thinking back on it now made him cringe.

"Aren't many left, thanks to folk like you. Soon none. Shame. We'll find something else, but still, it's a shame," said the seaman with a sullen, even tone.

Why was Armstrong telling him this? "Twenty-odd natural history museums have never needed thirty-six dead birds from Eldey," said Gus.

"You people pay a lot for skins and eggs," said Armstrong.

"Doesn't stop you from cracking those eggs for dinner."

"Used to be plenty in Newfoundland. We made a bad habit of taking the birds back then, but not much we can do about that now. They're tasty—meat that sticks to your ribs," he said. "Folk like you want to buy them off us, so we figure we can eat some of them and keep a couple for you, except there aren't many left now."

Gus felt weary. He had come to unwind like the others

with their pints, the men who didn't have auks at home, who weren't weighing moral questions about the origin of the feathers in their pillows or the omelettes on their plates, or contemplating the number of water jugs or baths a sea fowl requires. He did not want to think about the great auk, at least not here, not now. Ever since the creature had arrived at his house, he had felt he was living on the outer reaches of life, complacent in the ambient lethargy. He used to enjoy talking to everyone. When he had boarded the fishing vessel, he had thought himself a sailor, fond of the crew even though he was not one of them, fond of thinking he could, if he wanted, set out with them on fierce journeys, weather storms, and land on unexplored shores.

With his captive animal, Gus felt he was living outside the law, which was untrue, and that he'd also fallen prey to his own kind of soft and sentimental thinking, which was in some ways even worse. He found it irksome, these regrets at having eaten that bite of auk on the boat.

As a child he had loved a dog, and they used to go hunting together. He had cried at its death, yet forgotten the animal once a spunkier pup took its place. He could not even remember if he'd given it a name. It would be the same with the auk. Once it left, he would have the satisfaction of having acted in the name of science and no tears would be shed.

"Where is it, then, your auk?" Armstrong had still not moved.

"At the house." As he said it, Gus regretted telling the truth. He took one sip, then several more, to try to relax.

Twenty minutes later, something compressed his ribs and restricted his breathing. Before it had been Einarsson, now the entire room felt oppressive, amid a group of men he now realized he would never belong to, one whose company he liked much better than Buchanan's, surprisingly. These were the people he should get on with, the people he should comprehend. Yet he felt far off, out of place, absurd in a room whose atmosphere was warm and inviting but frightening as well. Everything made him anxious: Einarsson's glances across the room, Armstrong's half-closed, almost cruel eyes.

Armstrong was a vicious man, of that he was sure. He had found him kind at first, but now realized it had been a mistake, that engaging in conversation had led him to blunder, since the man was only after his auk. How naive he was, what a rank amateur. No one mixes with sailors so trustingly, even Cook surely didn't drink at the tavern with them. He had thought himself lethargic before, but only by comparison with the brutality that he could feel about to erupt around him. He sipped his beer, if only to compose himself.

A scuffle broke out near the door. Half an hour must have passed. He did not turn around right away, taking his cue from the others at the table. Soon something was smashed: a glass or a chair leg. He was not surprised, as he knew the violence of mariners first-hand. At the same time, thanks to this last beer, he was less anxious and had mostly gone back to feeling fondly toward these mariners and their short-fused, deadly solemn ways. He thought of *Last of the Mohicans,* wondering if the men in the room, the oldest of them at least, had ever seen the Iroquois on the shores of Canada. He had been captivated by that book. Though it was only a short time ago, he had been young and inexperienced, unlike now when he could be found lurking in notorious places such as this one. He chuckled to himself, thinking of how far he had come from his pharmaceutical studies in Lille to this hole in the wall at the far reaches of an austere archipelago.

He did not know the name of the lad who had sat down next to him. Nor could he ask, since the boy must have told him going on a dozen times now. Gus's tongue had turned to cement—a common occurrence during long conversations in English. Unless it was the drink. What was certain was the boy was much younger than Armstrong, twenty-four or twenty-five, around the same age as Gus. His freckles gave him the tinge of a setting sun. He seemed to be speaking about Canada and the Hurons, or no, it was Gus who was speaking about the Hurons, and the boy simply smiled warmly and chatted with the people next to him. He was charming and good-natured, though, laughing at every sentence Gus uttered and encouraging the rest of the table to do the same.

Gus wondered where the devil Armstrong had disappeared to. If he were here now, before this captive audience, that old sailor would stop putting on irritating airs of superiority with him. Then there Armstrong was again; incredible, that tonight all of Gus's thoughts came true. Armstrong gripped Gus's arm and brought his face up close. Gus could see he meant no harm. It was a gesture of acknowledgement between adventurers perhaps, a sign of reconciliation surely. What was he saying? He didn't understand much, but the words "home" and "drunk," or something else uttered in English stood out from the rest. Of course, he was saying he should go home and that he was drunk. They could say what they would, but even drunk he understood English. Gus got up and Armstrong moved to help him. He refused, while thinking how he had been wrong to doubt the man before. Armstrong was loyal, kind to his comrades.

When Gus left the tavern, he was happy. He had spent a pleasant evening in the company of these proud and valiant men. The air had a slightly sobering effect, but on walking in the door, and going up the stairs, his opinion endured.

He woke late the next day, exhausted by his night out. He had a sore throat; he kept replaying the image of the fight that hadn't involved him, the faces of men listening to him talk, trying hard to read their expressions, mocking or empathetic. Gus was not used to drinking, least of all with sailors.

He mustered the effort, though bothersome, to get up and go down to the study. Even more vexing, he had to leave his bedroom out of a duty to the auk, whose hunger did not, at that moment, impress Gus as a burning priority.

The auk cried when it saw him, pattered over to him as quickly as it could, or at least it seemed so to Gus. The sound had been brief, like a peal of relief at the joy of not having been forgotten. It then struck Gus that to be waited for by a creature who was nearly as unknown as a stranger in the street, yet who bestowed on him so naturally, so universally in a way, such attention and affection, even self-serving, was touching. It seemed to him that the auk had human expressions, a glint in its eye that signified "you're finally here," its neck moving forward and adding, "I missed you." When it brushed its beak against the leg of his pants, Gus was overcome with emotion.

The auk was hungry. Its wings erected, it was pacing between Gus and the back wall where Gus usually fed it. It shifted its weight from right to left, as always, but more dexterously this time. Today, the auk seemed like a goose frantic to restore order to a barnyard in the throes of anarchy. Gus felt tender toward it, in all its vulnerability, in a way he had not anticipated, a shameless admission of dependence on another creature with which he shared no common custom.

It was not love, or friendship, or even affinity. The word clicked once he formulated the thought: It was *responsibility*. Until now, he had only felt a sense of responsibility toward his mother, a widow who had pinned all her hopes and dreams of happiness on her son, coddling him throughout his studies and keeping a watchful eye on his career prospects. The care he gave the auk was unconditional, with no expectation of gratitude or future complicity, unlike with his mother, whom he was forever afraid of disappointing. He had to help the auk, feed it, bathe it, because he had chosen it one day, because he alone had decided to take the creature captive, and also—and most importantly—because the animal asked it of him, and it was a frail creature, helpless, injured, and very much *alive*.

Gus watched the auk gobble its fish, swallowing loudly and letting out little satisfied cries, and he understood that without him this living creature would die. An imperative all the more urgent due to insurmountable differences: They would never speak to nor understand one another; the only thing connecting them was an intuitive understanding of life, which they both wished to preserve. Gus was responsible for the great auk. For the way it took a fish in its beak, though Gus himself used cutlery, for how it plumed its feathers, though he had none, for the urge to dive under water, himself unable to swim. It destabilized him even further to know he was responsible for a creature he did not understand, that was not one of his own making nor an invention of past generations, a creature that had never needed someone like him before. He could stomach disappointing his mother, this he already knew and accepted as a possible outcome, one he did not fear as much as she did—if he did disappoint her, he could always try reminding her that it is foolishness for a seafarer's mother to be disappointed in her son—and while that, too, he could live with, he could under no circumstances accept betraying the trust of a creature unable to respond, or to understand if he responded.

At that moment, something swelled up inside him, no doubt aided by the lingering alcohol. An emotion fissured his whole being like a veinous arborescence expanding outward from the navel and across his shoulders. He wished the very best for the great auk. And he hoped that one day the auk would come up to him again and rub its beak against his leg, unprompted by the fear of starvation.

HE WOULD NOT SET FOOT IN THE TAVERN AGAIN, NOR wake past seven in the morning. One day, he finally found a reply from Garnier in the letter box. Its mere presence bespoke his imminent departure from Stromness, whatever the great auk's destiny turned out to be: a caged creature alive and sailing to France or a skin flattened and rolled like parchment to be stuffed at a later date.

He did not wish to open the letter at the post office as it was clear that, given the matter at hand, reading it would require a more private and serious setting. Out on the narrow street—narrow being the defining characteristic of all the streets in Stromness—he told himself the rain would be distracting and decided to return at once to the house, on the other side of town. But the letter burned a hole in his pocket, and he was too impatient to wait. He leaned against a wall to get out of the rain, which was really the sole advantage of a street so narrow, and opened the letter, skimming it quickly at first. Garnier asked him to return to Lille at once with the bird, dead or alive, whatever was possible, it was for him to decide. A whole paragraph was dedicated to the prestige the great auk would bring the museum. Every major establishment was in search of one. Paris did not have one—*yet*, he emphasized—the only one in France was in Strasbourg, a donation from Russia in 1760, when the great auk was far less rare. Gus folded the letter up again. He had read enough, he would finish the rest in the quiet of his own home.

So he would be leaving soon. He walked down the long

road, taking a left at the next fork to get a view of the city from the bay. This took all of two minutes since Stromness was so small. In one blink he took in the entire minuscule town. The dreary pink granite houses that could have looked bright were instead austere. Something about the scenery, this hill looking down to the port, with only a few lone houses, had an air of sadness, of disappointment, as though the town itself knew something were lacking. From the day he arrived, he had felt the monotony provoked by the dull, defeated landscape. He tried to visualize some improvements. The light was likely too diluted once it reached here. Then he realized what it was: There were no trees, since they could not grow in such strong winds.

At the idea of seeing Stromness for one of the last times, he tipped toward an indulgent state of mind. Heading once more toward the house, he felt a surge of nostalgia for all he could still lay eyes on. Perhaps it was not as boring as all that. Yes, some trees would have added a little liveliness, whimsy, and varied hues, but stark severity did have a certain charm, after all. No doubt he would remember it when he was far from here. He would remember Buchanan, too, with whom he had gotten on so well. He should go see Buchanan, in fact, as Buchanan should be the first to know of his departure. He did not self-inflict the cruelty of noting that, in any case, apart from Buchanan and Mrs. Bridge, he had no one else to inform.

He doubled back. The road grew steeper, the rain less copious. Buchanan was at home and had no doubt just finished shaving, since Gus noted a scrape bleeding near his Adam's apple. He was getting ready to go out. Gus walked with him to the harbour. Right away, he told him about the letter. Buchanan congratulated him, reddening and clapping him on the shoulder like the young men they still were.

"You'll be missed."

And Gus thought that he would not miss Buchanan, but that he would be happy to one day cross paths again in a faraway city where the weather was warm and everything quite different from what either of them knew.

"You'll miss the auk more than me, I suppose," Gus said, to be polite.

"I was going to say...why don't you leave it with me. It's silly for you to bring the bird with you. It's a death sentence. Better to set it free—the two of us together, or I could do it alone after you leave."

"That's impossible. I have to bring it back with me."

"You could always say it escaped."

Buchanan walked at his usual quick pace. Gus worried about slipping down the steep wet hill.

"What good is a stuffed bird? There's already one in Strasbourg, you said so yourself. And they must have dozens in Edinburgh and London..."

They arrived at the harbour. Boats were setting out on the water, others were unloading cargo, children ran around. A man came over to Buchanan and asked him a question. Buchanan answered, gestured something, and the man hurried over to some barrels stored on the quay. Gus observed, stunned. This sensitive reed of a man he thought he knew had become someone firm, direct, and respected. Gus, despite the bustle, kept talking. When Buchanan answered, his expression changed, and Gus thought his eyes looked like the moody pools of Stromness. No doubt his presence embarrassed Buchanan while he was working, since he declared they would discuss it later, when he passed by at the usual hour, and he added: "In the meantime, please think it over. Ask yourself what exactly is accomplished by sending such a rare animal to France, where it can't reproduce."

Others arrived to speak with Buchanan. He was apparently indispensable to the industrious town of Stromness.

No, Gus would not consider Buchanan's proposal, which violated his agreement with the Museum of Lille. He hurried home, rushing as the man on the quay had, but in his case due to a foul mood. He looked straight ahead. He felt no more nostalgia for this damp hole in the ground. A man knocked into him. Not by accident, thought Gus, but at that moment it didn't matter to him either way. Finally he walked through the front door, and upon entering saw the study door ajar, and as he got closer he could see Mrs. Bridge through the opening, bent down before the bird with something in her hand, which she offered it. They looked at one another intently: the creature eating, the woman watching it as it ate. When Gus stepped forward, Mrs. Bridge heard the sound, and Gus saw her stand back up, the auk at her feet, its neck craning toward her in surprise. She smoothed her apron and, before Gus could ask her anything, explained that she was doing some much-needed tidying up in there. Her taut chin furrowed like a worn-out sieve as she spoke. She must have read Gus's poor mood in his expression, since she immediately changed her story: In fact, she had heard the bird crying.

"Crying?" repeated Gus, suspicious.

"Aye, it was crying. Why, does that surprise you?"

"I've never heard it 'cry' before."

"Call it what you like. It was unhappy shut in here alone. I came to comfort it."

"I thought you hated it."

"There's not a thing on this earth I hate. As if I had the time to go around hating things!"

The auk brushed up against her skirts, letting out pleading cries; Mrs. Bridge swatted it away with a hand she tried to keep firm, but which became soft and gentle as it neared the bird. Straightening up, she shrugged with her chin lifting toward the ceiling and her eyes following suit toward an invisible sky and, as though it were usual for her limbs and features to levitate separately from the rest of her body, left the room in a disjointed state, rag in hand.

These Scots complicated his life immeasurably. Now apparently Mrs. Bridge was concerned the seabird was unhappy, whereas she would gladly have served it for supper two weeks ago. And Buchanan took himself for a zoologist with all his talk about what was best for a wild animal. The auk could not tell, but Gus was giving it the cold shoulder, the same treatment afforded to Mrs. Bridge, and Buchanan, and anyone else wishing to make him feel guilty in some way or another.

He opened the letter again. Garnier's excitement was palpable. He congratulated Gus repeatedly and, as everyone had commented ever since Gus took an interest in the subject, underlined the bird's rarity—one perpetuated by the laying of a single egg each year, rendering the population's renewal precarious. What's more, in 1775, the government of Newfoundland outlawed the capture of great auks, though without success. Garnier hoped Gus understood the import, for the field of science, of the animal in his possession. Then came the practical details: Gus would take a boat for Dunkirk—there were many—and a carriage would meet him there and take him to Lille. Garnier would have a basin built for the bird to swim in.

Gus rested the letter on his thigh, too tired to get up. He looked at the auk, with its head stock-still and straight, eyes closed, facing the wall. Its body rose and fell. It was breathing, not in itself a surprising fact, but one he found moving nonetheless. The bird was alive, it had reflexes just like him, needed air like him, and if deprived of that air, the bird would suffer and suffocate with equal violence. It could be said they were not all that different from one another. Except Gus, to be fulfilled, had to pursue a career, build a future, get married. There was a whole world, full of unknown fauna, waiting for people like him. He could not sacrifice everything for a bird.

"The whole thing's absurd. Everything about it. You might as well have left the bird to get plucked to death on Eldey."

Buchanan had arrived at five, as usual.

And as usual, he was correct.

"Find him a female auk, let them reproduce…"

What was Buchanan talking about? Gus was not about to start building an ark.

"Why a female? How do you know the bird is male?"

Buchanan admitted it was true he did not know for certain. Gus was disappointed. He would have liked to know the animal's sex, but without other birds to compare it to, the differences were unknown. His auk's size was its size and that was all.

Later, once Buchanan had gone, Gus and the auk went to the beach. For ten days, hc had been using a boat he had bought to bring the bird swimming in deeper waters, when the sea permitted. He had staked a post in the ground and would tie the auk there as he pushed off the boat. He rowed out a few metres, released the auk into the water, and let it go out farther, on the end of the cord. What was the use of sending the bird to France if it would not be able to reproduce? None at all. The auk was there, at his mercy. It would live or die, depending on Gus's decision. And Gus, too, would succeed or fail at life, depending on whatever destiny befell the bird.

The auk pulled less on its cord now when he took it swimming. It seemed it was adapting to Gus's will, that his presence reassured it, as if the bird could measure the danger of fishers or small orca it might encounter. For the moment, it floated on the water, beak pointed skyward, neck pulled in, a position that looked at once awkward and droll. From time to time, one eye would glance over at Gus, head perfectly still, and it would open its beak, and Gus thought of this as the warmest of auk smiles.

Seeing the bird on the water like this, or rather, them seeing each other, he on the boat, the auk fifteen metres off, happy and resting, he felt they were a team, or maybe even friends. The bird's eye turned milky in the water. He had never noticed it before purchasing the small skiff, and he wondered if it was the sun reflected off the water, the muted colours of the sky and sea blending across the creature's iris. He liked the way it turned opaque all at once. At one point, he thought he saw a curtain pull across an imaginary rod from one side of the eye to the other. Sometimes the auk dove into the water, no doubt to swallow a fish or two. Sometimes when it emerged again, Gus could see its neck bulge, and a ball descend from its beak down its throat.

They had been in the water for a long time. Gus's hands were frozen. Why did he feel so uneasy? He came back to the shore and wound the cord back around the post, brought the boat up onto the beach, and sat down with his back against it. For the first time ever, Gus did not have to pull on the cord to bring the auk back by force, disentangling it from a wave. The auk moved slowly at first, then stepped more quickly once out of the water, agile though wobbly, letting out a single, sharp cry brief as a bullet's path—a cry of joy, in essence. And as though struck by that bullet, Gus found between his breast and his arm, in the fold of his coat, the bird's beak, the bird's body shiny with wetness, and he felt the heat from this body near his heart.

Gus did not dare move for fear of interrupting this moment where a wild creature had perhaps mistaken him for one of its own kind. He was sure he could hear the auk purring, a ridiculous thought since great auks, of course, do not purr; nonetheless, the fact was, it was indeed emitting a diffuse purring sound, softer than a pigeon's coo, a sound that rolled over on itself with hoots of interruption.

He did not know if two seconds or five minutes had passed when he moved his hand to rest gently on the animal's head. He slid it down to the neck and, at the end of this precautious route, reached the back, nearly warm and pulsating, between two spread wings, and let the two fingers move to its chest. He could no longer tell wet from dry, hot from cold. He could no longer smell the sea. The rocks beneath him no longer hurt. A living creature was surrendering—to him, the one who had torn it from its existence, who the bird now trusted.

The auk kept still, at least for a time, the length of which Gus was again unable to determine. Everything was calm, devoid of hostility, or even unpleasantness. He had everything he needed: fish to eat, water to drink, an animal to study, wind to cool him, a fireplace to warm up by. Rather than send the bird to France, with all the risks it implied, Gus had a duty to study the bird's movements and seasonally induced changes. He felt Garnier would agree. He saw no reason that could justify a refusal.

The auk pulled away and went back to walk on the rocks. Gus watched the creature, who was well-fed thanks to him, who had chosen him and depended on him. He would have liked to have called it over to nestle back into his arm, or so it would smile at him again. He remembered that he still had no idea if the bird were male or female. What a shame the French language offered no neutral form of address. What did he usually say? He thought of it as "the great auk" or "the animal" or "bird," and in his mother tongue these words were always masculine, perhaps the reason he took it for a male. Had he adopted a whale, *une baleine,* he would have no doubt imagined it as female; had he spoken to the bird in English, he might never have cared to wonder.

The bird had stopped, it was resting on the rocks, sitting up straight, firmly situated on its feet. It turned its head to Gus, then to the horizon and back, as though the two of them were commenting on the landscape. The seabird seemed to be showing Gus its vast domain, of an immensity and depth Gus could not even fathom, the grey expanse above them, for him only an ominous overcast sky. All of it belonged, or had belonged, to the bird. All of it had belonged to a bird that now belonged to Gus. A great auk no longer just a great auk, but *his* great auk, with whom he shared the waves, the beach, the strong gust of glacial winds, the softness of a rare break in the clouds, the hardness of the rocks. A great auk he wanted to name so he could call to it, as you call to a cat or a dog, or to a parrot, a kind of cousin flying above a canopy unknown to the human eye, just as a great auk dives down to the abyssal depths of the sea.

Gus stood up. As he walked over to the bird, he tried to think of a name. On the first step, he thought Neptune, after the god. On the second, he thought Tethys, like the goddess. And on the third, Dominique, a French name of no defined gender. On the fourth, he sought an adjective. And by the fifth, as he stood in front of the auk, he had it.

He stooped and picked up the bird to bring it home. He would call it Prosperous, because its round stomach evoked prosperity, after all, and because it was an English word that the French could understand and a name that hinted at impending happiness. Prosp for short, like Gus for Auguste.

A week had passed. He had sent Garnier his proposal. The day before, Buchanan had noted a surprising change on the auk: The white spots under each eye had disappeared, or were fading at least, yet the white feathers on the bird's body covered most of its head, lending it a more affable appearance. Gus had already witnessed the change at the beginning of his time with the bird. He and Buchanan were unsure why it was happening. Their only thought was that it was a side effect of captivity or a seasonal shift in plumage. In reality, as Gus would later learn, the two marks signified a reproductive period.

Gus disliked this change, which gave Prosp the aspect of a demure goose. When he looked at the bird straight on, if it was dark, its head disappeared into the night, while before two saucers formed frightening oblong holes, even in the dark. Presently it resembled a tropical plant, a stick of dry wood where two mushrooms might have grown. After this discovery, Gus spent much of the day drawing this progression. He was drawing for Garnier, for science, but also for pleasure, for the sake of happiness, or if not happiness then for a reasonable existence for himself and Prosp.

Except, a bearable life on Stromness seemed increasingly unlikely. Maybe he was imagining things, but since running into Einarsson, he'd formed an impression that the sailor's indignation at a perceived costly fancy was a sentiment widely shared on the island, one that resonated with its residents: Animals should be sold, eaten, or put to work. Before meeting Prosp, Gus would mostly have agreed, with the exception of exotic birds like parrots or parakeets, as poetic interior decor. It was true that Prosp lacked their beautiful colours.

For some time now, when he walked around Stromness, people would hush on his approach. The women gave him sideways glances, squinting warily. They would speak to him only to sell him some item at twice its worth; cheating him brazenly, demanding astronomical sums for mere trinkets—a knife, or candle that he had just watched someone else buy at its usual price. Gus pretended not to notice. It may have been foolish not to fight back, to let it slide, but he was afraid. People soon grew even bolder, asking him for news of his "beast." Rhetorically, of course, in a mocking and vaguely threatening tone. One day a man stared right at him and mimed twisting a chicken's neck, turning his two fists at the height of his navel. He was leaning against a wall opposite the grocer that Gus had just left. As he laughed, Gus could see a black row of rotting teeth.

On evenings when he wanted company, Gus would go to the few pubs frequented by mariners passing through who had never heard of him or his great auk. Never had he imagined having an entire community's loathing directed at him. Buchanan, who had warned him against the mariners, at first thought it would blow over. As did Mrs. Bridge, until one day she found a short-eared owl nailed to the front door. She began to wheeze and shake, unable to touch the thing. Gus took it down, and spent a half hour washing his hands. He was not afraid; he wanted blood.

He decided to leave. It would be pointless for him to end up in the paper's crime section, be it as murderer or victim. For once, Buchanan agreed. He suggested the Outer Hebrides, since it wasn't terribly far away and the climate was pleasant. Buchanan would happily visit Gus there.

"Of course, you'll have to set up in a village, somewhere even smaller than here, where you won't bother anyone."

"Where Prosp won't, you mean..."

"Yes. It shouldn't be hard. It's rather desolate out that way."

The details had to be arranged. Garnier had not replied to his letter, so Gus found himself without funds, except for the advance for the return to France, which he certainly intended to keep. He would have to write to his mother. Truth be told, she did not have much of an income. But Gus would ask for her help for a few months, at least. He would give his word he would repay her, of course, once he had carried out this grand endeavour and gotten all it would earn him: the money but also the fame. It would be some time till he could see her again, but she had to trust him; all mothers of great explorers lose sight of their children, spend years waiting on the docks. He knew that his mother, an adorable woman he loved and admired, would sacrifice herself for him in a second if necessary. And he was perfectly sincere in his talk of future repayment and fame.

He looked for a boat headed for the Outer Hebrides. There weren't many; he wondered about Canada. He found a Hudson's Bay Company ship set to sail with a cargo of freight and Scottish emigrants in fifteen days' time. He and Buchanan went over the plans for entire afternoons.

At times Gus thought Buchanan would have liked to go with him but lacked the courage to leave everything behind. They spoke of Prosp, watched Prosp, sketched Prosp. From their observations, they developed theories about great auks and penguins, and wild animals in general. For hours they discussed what domesticated animals had the ability to convey. Both mentioned dogs they knew who were exceptionally loyal companions. Gus remembered how Rousseau had been devastated by the death of his own dog; this led naturally to the application of this manner of seeing pets to the great auk, then they began to muse about the large species of wild animals in Africa and India. And what did they really know about the family life of tigers? Or why elephants live in groups?

Buchanan, who had never seen a giraffe—Gus had once,

in Paris—had difficulty imagining how one would walk. Gus described it as reed-like; Buchanan pictured a blade of grass in the wind, then applied that movement to the animal in the engraving before him, and the creature began to quiver in his imagination, to twist on its hooves before transforming into a heron tall as a roof ladder. He suspected he might be far off the mark. Gus was struggling to imagine a rhinoceros. Though he had read detailed descriptions, he kept picturing it with a turtle's shell. A pity he could not grasp its weight, or how much air moved when it walked. His fingertips itched, as tactile contact with Prosp had impressed upon him just how vital touch was, how without feeling the thickness of the skin, where the plumage began, the length of the feathers, he could not fully come to understand the auk. He and Buchanan wrote at length about the conclusions that could be drawn from Prosp, or the study of Prosp, and applied to other animal species.

They sat admiring the earth's abundance. The more they thought, the more they were awestruck by the miracle of the infinite variances in form that seemed to hint at some secret order. But unlike the mysteries they had revered as children, something here was stranger and more striking than divine design. Everything they looked at seemed to be driven by inner workings, with unique causes and consequences, leading to other causes and consequences, and so on, as science showed, though without a concrete explanation: a world with its own rules, nearly chemical in nature, logical as water turning to vapour at boiling point or an object falling to the floor when released, an autonomous order stemming from the very presence of a species and of protean plants, something independent and self-sustaining, subject to perpetual influences. Except they were ignorant of the conditions and sometimes wondered how many years had needed to pass for Prosp's ancestors to wake up one day flightless.

"We should find a companion for Prosp," said Buchanan one night, phrasing it this way to avoid the confusing question of the great auk's sex.

"Prosp is a priest, cassock and all," replied Gus.

"It doesn't make you uneasy, after all our discussion, to separate Prosp from the rest of his kind?"

"You said it yourself: If I abandon the bird now, it'll be more likely to end up in a pot of boiling water than warming an unbroken egg somewhere."

Patches of red appeared on Buchanan's cheeks, his lower neck, and the middle of his forehead, where the hives became a straight upwards line stretched out thin.

"That's my opinion," said Gus, "I don't want to make you angry. It's funny how you're so fixated on this companion business."

The blood seemed to rush into Buchanan's spots even more, and he now, comically, resembled an old maritime map with two vast continents facing one another, on either side of his nose, a pole around the roots of his hair.

"Are you all right?" Gus ventured.

"I'm going to be married. What I mean is...perhaps that's why I've spoken of...Prosp's solitude."

He clearly could not bring himself to say, "Prosp's sexuality."

Gus felt strange on hearing the news. He found himself absurd with his notebook of methodology of animal studies. It was as though a friend who had just celebrated his seventh birthday, under the pretext of having reached the age of reason, was leaving him, at the age of six, alone to play with toys that yesterday were still amusing. It was odd, but Gus felt betrayed, abandoned with Prosp and their adventure.

After a few seconds of silence, he congratulated Buchanan. What else could he do?

"Come visit us in Canada," said Gus, forcing a happy lilt at the end of the sentence.

Such was the order of things: marriage, a bourgeois life, and children, no doubt. In truth Gus had never considered travelling to the far reaches of the world with Buchanan and Prosp, yet the thought of a less conventional life, of having a partner in this strange tale, had been a pleasant one. Reassured, Buchanan paled again and promised that yes, he would visit. He said that everyone had a destiny to fulfill, one bestowed by nature. He had to marry, just as Gus would one day, and Prosp would very soon. Then his face grew red again.

After Buchanan's departure, things proceeded in their usual order: the cord, the wood post, the boat, the sea, the return to the beach, the post again, the boat pulled ashore. Then a whiteout, or a blackout rather, a terrifying and painful blow to the head, and, after, a fall and a rock from the beach striking his shoulder. He felt as though he were asleep, exhausted from gasping for air. He tried to move his leg, but it was too heavy, and to bring his hand to his forehead, but it was frozen in place. His mind whirred and abstract images flashed by: crossed wires in his brain, twisted veins pulsing in his neck. Finally he opened his eyes, and as if his eyes could hear, Prosp's panicked cries echoed in his aching skull.

A man was running down the beach, his ear bleeding, his curved back pressed against the auk to hold it fast and shield himself from its pecking. But he failed. Grabbing on to an animal flailing for its life is next to impossible. It seemed the man did not wish to kill the bird, or he would have done so by now. He tripped. Gus, still on his back but with his eyes open, thought he recognized Einarsson's peacoat and flat brown hair. The auk freed itself from the man's arms and, suddenly upright on two feet, darted toward the boat and diverted down the shoreline, chest puffed out, belly under it, shrieking with its beak wide open. Einarsson may have been an expert in killing great auks, but he had no idea how to capture a frenzied living, biting, scratching sea fowl. Nonetheless, he took off in pursuit.

Gus managed to get onto all fours. Pushing his right leg against the stern of the boat, he tried to stand up, but fell over again. When he finally managed, there was no sign of Prosp. Black spots in the form of nets smeared across his vision, as though he were behind broken glass. Einarsson ran back and forth in front of the rocks to the left of the beach. Gus hobbled toward him, propped up on an oar. Gus now saw that, before that moment, he had clearly never truly known what it meant to hate someone.

There was the quiet thud of wood to the skull. Einarsson lay in a puddle between some rocks, his mouth agape to the sky. His torn earlobe was bleeding again. When Gus saw Prosp step out of the crevice where it had been hiding, he passed out, on his back as well, a safe distance from the sailor.

It was the auk that woke Gus. It was biting at his nose, which did not hurt, only pinched, as the bird cut off his breathing then released its hold. It was, in fact, this apnea that woke Gus. The next day he would find two little holes encircled with bruises where the bird had bitten. Still groggy, Gus, who did not wish to end up a wanted man, began to worry about Einarsson. He must still be alive, as there was no trace of a body. It might have been washed away by the waves, though that was quite unlikely.

He and Prosp stayed there by the sea for some time, without touching or moving, Gus on his back and staring at the sky, the bird standing and looking out at the horizon. Gus knew he had no choice but to leave the next day, and that he might have little say in their destination. And that is how he ended up in the Faroe Islands, a place he never before had considered going.

II

HE LEARNED TO EAT WHALE MEAT AND RAN WITH the sheep through the austere landscape of black and green. He sailed on boats and watched an orca devour a seal near the beach one day. He thought about how the seal could have been Prosp, if Prosp was free to come and go and did not belong to him.

He spent his time watching Prosp, drawing Prosp, writing about Prosp. Each of the bird's movements was recorded, classified, archived. He knew more about the great auk than any other human on earth in the year 1836. He sent Garnier letters and kept him apprised. And Garnier had become resigned to this solution. In any case there was no menagerie in Lille, and Gus would never have accepted to give Prosp to Jardin des Plantes in Paris.

Since his arrival he had fallen in love, married, and could now be mistaken for a man of the Faroes. Elinborg, his wife, watched over Prosp with him. No one wholly understood each other. The bird because it was a bird, and his wife because she spoke to him in Danish, which he hadn't fully mastered yet, and the local Faroese, which he still stumbled over. Her home latitude was as exotic to him as the Amazon, the sky and sea creating a stifling atmosphere that he imagined similar to that of the endless rainforest. Sometimes he watched Elinborg sleep. She was strong and beautiful, her hair fine as Prosp's feathers but yellow as a canary's. Her hand clasped the sheet below her bare shoulder, her palm was red, the back of her hand, just like the rest of her, white, though summer brought a copper tinge, no doubt because of the wind.

In her sleep her lips pursed into a pout. She looked like both the most serene and the most vulnerable creature he had ever seen, and he wondered what she was dreaming of, what kinds of landscapes her mind could create when all she'd ever seen were high cliffs overlooking waves so icy she'd never dream of dipping in even a toe, and grassy hills with nothing to distract the eye, so that she had no knowledge of the nature of a forest, or even a tree, as the entire archipelago was bereft. Elinborg had left Tórshavn, the island's sole and minute major town, for a village with a dozen houses, for Gus—and for Prosp. Together they had built a basin and fenced it off, even though in front of the house, in front of everyone's houses here, a beach stretched out, where in the evening he'd bring the auk swimming.

The sand was black, much more pleasant than the rocks of the Orkney Islands. Every time Gus walked across the dirty, almost oily ground, he thought of Elinborg, who would never know shores like those he'd seen in France, like at Dunkirk where the beach was pale and sometimes even glowed under the light of the blue sky for days on end—a marvel unknown to his wife. Prosp, for the last few months, had gone walking ahead or behind him on the shore, each at their own pace as it were, before plunging into the water. The bird knew elements and landscapes foreign to Gus too; the depth of the ocean, the underwater shadows of the whales, the clouds of herrings, the gusting storms, things that were, in fact, more familiar to Elinborg than to him. When Prosp swam, Gus no longer really watched over him. He would doze instead, or take out a book, the cord looped around his ankle and his back resting against the rocks at the edge of the grass; he raised a tarp on stakes he had driven into the ground, to protect him from the rain while he waited for his great auk to return to shore.

Sometimes Gus wondered if he still saw Prosp as a great auk, a bird, a mysterious creature or at any rate one completely foreign to him, that understood him no better than he understood it, though it possessed an acute comprehension of his morphology and expressions. Gus spent so much time caring for the bird that sometimes he felt they were both unsure who was who, that each of them was an extension of the other. Going outside accompanied by this boot-high feathered appendage had become as natural as wearing a hat; saying "come" to this bird had become as normal as opening the door for Elinborg when they went out.

It seemed ridiculous when he thought about it, but he believed he had acquired the spirit of a great auk. He hadn't spoken of it to anyone, not aloud and above all not in his correspondence, but he believed he could feel what Prosp felt. When the auk was annoyed, it displayed its ill humour by remaining perfectly still, standing up on its feet, eyes half-closed, with the omniscient air of a vengeful totem. Gus tried in vain to coax Prosp with gentle words, but the auk, stock-still and furious, would not budge. If Gus took out his sketchbook anyway, Prosp's hieratic pose left much to be desired. It seemed almost that the bird was acting like a stone on purpose, just as a child sent to their room will also refuse to eat the food brought to the door on a tray. If, in an effort to make Prosp give in, Gus opened the gate to the pen and began walking the path to the beach—the path toward an irresistible swim—the auk would turn just its head around and give Gus an undeniably scornful look as it watched him take a few steps, as though never in all its days had it observed a movement so absurd.

After, taking on a weary air—or worse, a condescending one—Prosp would start slowly down the path to the beach, neck straight and bill held high, not toward the sky, which indicated a pleasant mood, but parallel to the ground. The auk walked along with a pendulous gait, tugged forward, unsteadied, by its bill, unaware of the kindly and comical air this gave it. It made Gus hope that Prosp's foul mood would last as long as possible. But then later, the excitement of the sea took over, and all was forgotten.

Gus was entering his second month of July on the Faroes when one morning Prosp began to cry non-stop. Gus thought at first that there must be an eagle flying over the pen, which always made Prosp panic and flee to the barn. But that day the auk did not hide, instead batting its wings, extending them away from its body and flapping them frantically, as if it was a wolf alerting its pack. Prosp then howled, head high, addressing the clouds. Gus worried his auk would choke as he watched the bird's narrow chest contract more and more with each breath.

When the auk saw Gus, it ran toward him, pecked his calf, then hurried off to do a lap around the pen. Gus tried to grab the bird but could not manage: Prosp kept biting him. For no apparent reason, no noise in particular, no cruel or dangerous birds circling above, no whales on the horizon, not even a rowdy child nearby (Prosp did not care for children). Already a neighbour was headed over, alerted no doubt by the cries but mostly exasperated. Gus apologized and the man, called Jakupsson, a fisherman from a village of farmers, looked at him, disappointed by how useless Gus was, and rolled his shoulders back as he continued to watch Gus's futile efforts to calm the beast. People there, Gus had noticed, were not keen to help you if your actions seemed to them of a kind with madness or costly, in money or energy.

Meanwhile Prosp kept crying out, and Gus kept running after Prosp. And Jakupsson stared at the auk, alert to its every expression. When Gus, who was quite worked up, asked if the man could help, Jakupsson uttered his first words of the morning: "Grab it from the side, by the neck. They can't turn around."

Gus understood enough to get the gist, aided by Jakupsson's gesture, his hand rounded like a hairpin. Which Gus found irritating since clearly the man's involvement stopped there, and he did not consider it his duty to run behind the bird to demonstrate. Gus, worn out, gave up.

"Strange beasts, those ones," said Jakupsson. "I've seen my fair share in the sea, a long time ago. I even caught one once, seems to me. They say they're witches. Maybe that's why you don't see them anymore."

"There's Prosp. And I've seen more of them toward Iceland."

"Still, seems you don't find them nowadays. Didn't know they could live so long out of the water," said Jakupsson, nodding his head for emphasis.

"What makes you say they're witches?"

"They'll call up a storm if you catch them at sea. When you get them on land, they can't do much. That's why they're all gone. They got caught on land. No more witches now."

Gus had already heard this tale of witches. All of a sudden, the atmosphere of calm, the sky empty of eagles, the tranquil water of the sea, and Prosp's frantic shrieking left him with a feeling of dread.

"Don't reckon yours is a witch. More like a chicken or a rooster. No offence. But it's the last one I'll see in my lifetime, I guess..."

Prosp was still running around, though losing speed until it halted altogether, exhausted. Jakupsson shrugged and got up as though at the end of an amusing performance or travelling attraction. He placed a finger on his hat to bid Gus farewell, and Gus did the same, standing alone as his neighbour's back grew smaller, next to an animal that seemed to want to catch its breath for a few minutes.

An hour later, Gus saw what Prosp had heard, or guessed, before him. The hill had been overtaken by the sounds of beasts melding into a single tone—minus the auk, which had quieted and hid in the barn. The sheep atop the hill were having their wool torn off with bare hands, some of it bloodied. The annual shearing had begun. Woolen tufts rained down like snow and drifted toward the village. The wind blew one onto Gus's neck. From afar it looked like dandelions turned to fluff, but when he removed the little hard, viscous clump from the base of his hair, a red mark smeared across his neck and stained his collar.

In that moment, Gus thought he saw parts of the sea take on a reddish hue. He would have liked to lie down on the ground and cover his ears, as one shelters from the impact of cannon fire. The sheep's bloody fleece landing on him brought on nausea, his mouth filled with the taste of fatty putrefaction. He did not wonder where Elinborg was; he knew that she would be inside, cleaning, unperturbed. Never again would he buy a shawl made on the islands, he vowed, feeling a surge of anger at his wife for being born in such a place, an anger all the more powerful because she was so oblivious. He suspected something barbarous or violent lay deep inside her, dormant perhaps but present nonetheless. The year before, the sheep shearing—for that was the name by which it must be called, in any case—must have taken place somewhere else on the island, where the sheep had wandered off to graze, since they were left to roam essentially free. How could he find a way to be off-island with Prosp next year, he wondered.

At the end of the day, silence fell. Gus had joined Prosp in the barn a few hours earlier. It was still light outside. And incredibly, the sheep, now calm, bleated peaceably. Elinborg called out to him, in the direction of the beach, where she thought he had taken Prosp, since it was time for the bird's swim. But for the rest of the day Prosp stayed at a distance. Gus could see the great auk's eyes glinting in the corner, from behind the trunk where it had wedged itself. It was again distrustful; people, no doubt, had proved disappointing. Gus did not try to approach. He understood. Agreed, even.

Gus had loved Elinborg, a merry young girl, from the moment he saw her in Tórshavn where she lived with her uncle, an official, and her aunt whom she helped with the children, no doubt while waiting to find a husband. At the table before the entire family, Elinborg kept interjecting, asking Gus questions about France and the museum, about anything and everything, so long as she could talk loudly and raise her eyebrows up to her forehead, which would crease in response, because every part of her ached for constant movement. Her parents lived on a farm, which on this desolate archipelago was as good a living as one could expect.

Tórshavn was a gloomy, impoverished town whose streets were too narrow for two horses to pass and whose houses—except the government buildings—were small wood-plank cottages the wind went right through. The people were handsome, and kind. After ten days Gus loved a place that had seemed detestable when he'd first arrived. He could not put his finger on the source of its charm. He figured it must be the dramatic, striking landscapes, or the effect of everything together: the blend of bitterness and warmth, the sentiment that the people there had blended with the open plains and the still, stony ground.

One man had explained to Gus in complete seriousness that he belonged to a family descended from a seal. The story was a well-known one in town: One of his ancestors had seen a seal turn into a woman on the beach. He fell in love at once, saved the woman, and took the sealskin she had abandoned on the beach and locked it inside a trunk. The two were married and had children. One day, while out fishing, he remembered too late he'd left the key to the trunk at home. His wife found the key, took back her sealskin, slipped it on, and swam back into the sea. The man told Gus this story as casually as he might say his father owned a shop in Tórshavn or that his daughter was recently married. Gus wondered if the story had resonated because of Prosp, or because of Elinborg.

After they were married, Gus and Elinborg settled in her family's village. Her white moon-shaped face resembled a luminous stone against the volcanic rock; she seemed almost elfin, quick-witted and mischievous like all elves, yet also grounded. He imagined she possessed the strength to stand on the edge of a cliff and face down a storm, her skirt flying in all directions and her hair pulled asunder by the winds while her body—her legs, arms, her torso—remained motionless. She had large hips, and he loved that about her. In bed at night, he would rest a hand on her hip and sleep pressed up against her bottom, which was higher than his own, and feel protected.

Several times each year, the village held celebrations. They danced a kind of slow farandole, miming old legends to a melody with barely two or three modulations. Their voices rendered an iron-like serpentine sound.

Gus had quickly gotten back to work. In addition to notes on the auk, Garnier wanted Gus to study the flora and fauna of the far north. In just under two years, Gus had published a good number of articles in journals: on dolphins and puffins, and on the flighted lesser auks known as razorbills, and on their flightless cousins, the great auk, with its atrophied wings. Not often exactly but once in a while Gus was invited to scientific conferences. He had to tear himself away from Prosp and Elinborg. He felt diminished without them, as though his entire being, right down to the last molecule, were only a poor sketch of a man. Some hurried and uncertain feeling seemed to follow him about; he felt incomplete. His detachable collar felt tight and itchy on his neck, the women he crossed paths with seemed tedious and false compared to Elinborg, who even in her petticoats could chase a sheep up a hill, and would discuss with him how species change over time as though she'd read Lamarck.

It happened that fall that he had to go to Denmark. At the University of Copenhagen, he met a man who kept a personal menagerie in Norway. Kroyer was barely older than Gus but had travelled a great deal. Now he was waiting on funding, readying himself to sail along the coasts of Jutland to survey the fish in Danish waters. This was very similar to what Gus's research entailed. In Copenhagen, Gus spoke in French, as most people spoke it. He was out of the habit, at least speaking out loud. He realized how the effort of speaking on the island wore out his throat; in French, his voice sang and whistled, danced, a breeze against his front teeth.

Gus spoke of Prosp. Kroyer listened with interest. He told Gus he'd not seen any great auks in some time. True, perhaps he wasn't visiting the right places; maybe Gus was correct to think the birds had moved farther north. In any case, everyone knew numbers were dwindling. Kroyer's theory was that the population was reaching the exact number needed for balance in the world. A hypothesis that, it must be said, annoyed Gus. There was something cynical, or perhaps resigned, about this idea of Kroyer's, something horribly counterintuitive in the idea that the disappearance of a species could lead to an "improvement," whatever that meant. He felt a malaise in his chest, which, for a reason he could not name, felt like an accusation of a failure to act, to tip the scales back instead of closing his eyes and accepting it as fact, as though Gus had just learned a plague would ravage a quarter of humanity, yet felt relief at the thought that there would now be fewer carriages clogging the streets of Paris, London, and Copenhagen.

When he arrived home, Gus found the house turned upside down. Prosp had been sulking, defiant, and even hostile toward Elinborg. While it hadn't bitten her, the auk had delivered a series of pecks—beak closed, at least—and had hidden when Elinborg approached the pen, and turned its back as though offended by the sight of her, refusing to eat the fish she brought until she left. Prosp hated her, she said, rather vexed. Yet Prosp had loved Elinborg once. Before the trip, every day the auk would run up to her when she went into the pen. She'd watch the bird swimming in the basin, and she'd laugh at the sight, and sometimes she'd go with them, Gus and Prosp, to the beach. In those moments, it seemed to Gus that Prosp acted differently, as though putting on a show, doing brilliant jumps into the water to dazzle them. And when the auk came back to shore, it would sit a couple of metres away, as though the three were old friends chatting at length as they picnicked on the icy shore.

But now everything had changed. When Gus came home, the auk threw itself at Gus's knees, yelping, then dashed to the gate of the pen. Gus brought Prosp to the beach, Elinborg following behind. Neither paid her much attention. There would be no happy family picnic that day. Gus, recharged by the trip and certain he would now produce important research, studied Prosp as though for the very first time. He did not so much as glance at his wife. And as for Prosp, the auk waited for her to leave to be with the only being of importance.

When Gus came back to the house after Prosp's swim, Elinborg was fiddling with the stove, her poker turning the cinders and logs one way then the other and then another; it seemed, thought Gus, as though she had never before witnessed combustion. She crouched down before it, and as Gus passed behind her, he rested a hand on the nape of her neck, pushing two fingers against her collarbone. Then he stooped to reach the back of her neck, where strands of her light hair had escaped from her bun and stuck to her skin in long snakes. But Elinborg shook her shoulders and got to her feet to fetch another futile log for the poker to rustle around.

"You can sit down," she said, grabbing the soup tureen, as the enamelled plate struck the wood table.

And that was all. At least at first.

"I'll go get Prosp if you like," she added.

Then Gus finally understood. When he sat down, he was aware something truly new was about to begin: his first fight with his wife.

He wanted to apologize. Yet he was surprised to find he could not figure out where to start.

"You can sleep with your bird, too, since you missed it so much," she huffed.

Gus wanted to say something gentle, but no easy phrase came to mind. The woman before him, red-cheeked from the fire, was unlike the Elinborg he knew. He was not afraid of her, nor did he find her displeasing, she was just different, a version of his wife he had yet to encounter. He was unsure what to do.

"Nothing to say to me, then? You think it's normal not to have a thing to tell me? No, I don't have feathers, sorry. I'm of no interest to the university. I could cluck-cluck-cluck, if you like?"

Elinborg, fists clenched against her chest, raised her

elbows and thrust them forward like stumps to the beat of an ever-strident crowing. Then, in a sudden grotesque farce, the sound became deafening, as she circled his chair, upright with her nose stuck forward, the stumps dancing around her, her ass high and thrust out too. Sweat beaded on her reddened forehead, her sleeves floated and skirted her cheeks, when suddenly she stopped and fell silent. She sat solemnly down and took up her usual posture in front of her plate.

"So, my friend, what did you get up to in Copenhagen?"

Of course, for Gus, a novice in disputes, the sarcasm went unnoticed. So after swallowing, he obliged, naively, unwittingly.

Elinborg listened to her husband but let his accounts fall one by one to the kitchen floor, more indifferent than if she had just dropped a hard-boiled egg from a plate. As Gus described Kroyer's menagerie, she shrugged, bored. When he spoke of Kroyer's trip to Greece, she rolled her eyes. When he told her that he, Gus, had been praised for one of his articles, he noticed she was crying.

It came as a shock, for he had never seen her cry before. It was the first time a woman had cried because of him, and he felt a sort of pride. The entire process fascinated him. He watched as her faced changed, twisted, complexified, her features deepening in disorder, the way the liquid ran down her cheek, how the tears formed in the corner of her eye. He waited for her nose to grow red and swollen and wet. Even her hair seemed to thin with sadness, by which he meant meagre patches of it had begun to cling to her sweaty forehead.

When she stood up in a clatter of dinnerware and ran up the stairs, which were perhaps more like a ladder, and into the bedroom, Gus felt stupid and cruel. He followed after her, so tired that he missed a step and landed at her feet, with his head against the mattress off of which her legs were swaying back and forth as she lay staring at the ceiling, so focused on the spot above her that she did not see his ridiculous posture, his twisted knee. He asked for forgiveness, and of course she granted it, because they loved each other.

Had his return been too abrupt for Prosp, or had Prosp suffered from his absence? Either way, the next day when Gus went to see the bird, it was lying curled up, unmoving on the ground in the corner of its pen. When Gus went over, the auk didn't even look up. The November wind lifted its feathers above its head, tousling its back. Gus went up and rubbed its neck. The auk let him, indifferent. Gus picked it up and realized Prosp's body was limp. He wondered if Prosp had a fever, and felt the bird's stomach in case. Prosp did not seem to notice. When Gus put the bird down, it took up its sullen posture again, and the wind once more ruffled its feathers. When Gus held out a fish, it did not open its beak, and when Gus placed the fish in front of it, it did not move. Gus snapped his fingers next to the bird's head in hopes of triggering a reflex, at the least, but the auk seemed to have gone deaf.

When an animal suffers, does it cry out? Are its complaints understandable to humans? Gus had no answer to these questions. He'd hunted, he'd seen animals on a farm, he'd had a dog, had met numerous cats. The dog had never once complained, the birds had been in good health until shot through with a bullet. Gus knew nothing of creatures sick or dying—he knew not to which category Prosp now belonged. Perhaps his auk simply had a melancholic temperament? Did animals have moods? They must, as dogs have been known to die of sadness. But what about penguins, or auks?

In the end, Prosp had gotten angry with Elinborg, and Gus knew it: Prosp had feelings, a personality replete with deep affections and hatreds.

He carried Prosp to the house. He wanted to settle the seabird into a warm corner and keep an eye on it. The drooping auk slipped its beak between his sleeve and his chest. The wind whipped around him, swept back his hat and left Prosp dishevelled. Though Elinborg would not be pleased to see Gus bring the bird into the house, she would allow it and take pity. Perhaps the two would even reconcile. And indeed, that was just what happened when she saw the pair walk through the door, and Gus placed Prosp in her arms and the bird just lay there. At the sight of the auk's limp body, Elinborg brushed away what was left of her jealousy, and as for Prosp, the auk did not have the strength for sentiments. They rested Prosp in a basket full of laundry. And Prosp looked Gus straight in the eyes—a rarity.

Never had Gus seen an expression so empty, so grave, so resigned. Prosp's eyes had taken on a milky hue, unless it was Gus's eyes misting over. It seemed as though the bird's dried-out feathers were about to fall out. Prosp emitted a small cry, as though the wicker of the basket were painful, then quieted. It looked at Gus, inquisitively, perhaps questioning the source of this weariness. It accepted Elinborg's damp hand on its back to smooth out the mess of plumage. Gus suddenly feared he was watching Prosp's final hours. Since the day he'd saved the auk on the island of Eldey, he'd taken on a responsibility; the auk, in its own way, had trusted Gus, had accepted a new way of life at his side, agreeing to bend to his will, to swim in the sea only when permitted, and in exchange Gus provided constant protection, food, the promise of survival.

While the auk knew not exactly how, it had been betrayed by Gus. That was the meaning of the look in the bird's eyes, stunned at what was happening. Why was Gus, in his position of total power, forsaking Prosp? Before, Gus had seen the bird's movements as a limpid translation of its feelings, the expression of instant joy on reaching the beach, of the auk's tranquil sleep, perfectly upright, its fear when an eagle appeared in the sky. Never had he wondered what Prosp was doing or feeling when he wasn't there observing, whether, for instance, the auk remembered the ocean, its existence before Gus. For Gus, Prosp was Prosp, an auk called Prosp, a unique specimen not to be confused with any other. He knew the shape of the bird's spots near its eyes come summer, he knew the precise colour of its feet, the chalky markings that would eventually appear.

And as for the auk, was it aware that Gus was a man, or Elinborg was a woman, for that matter? Did he think the house a nest, or an isle? The auk, after all, did not know its own appearance, did not know it was an auk, that it was black with a large white spot across its belly. Perhaps it believed it was the only one of its species, or even that it was human. Why, in fact, would it believe any different? Gus spoke to Prosp, making sounds as though in response. Just as Gus didn't understand the language of auks, Prosp did not understand his either, and yet Gus was convinced they could understand each other, that in among the vastness of their respective vocabularies, they had found common modulations, tones, and inflections. Why wouldn't the auk have thought itself human? Why didn't Gus believe himself an auk? Was the bird even aware of whether it was happy or sad? Gus felt that the sole fact of being alive should have made it happy, yet his seabird lived unaware of the safety its pen provided each day from rorquals, ungrateful of the advantages of living near Gus, with daily feedings guaranteed, and safety. Yet would Gus have sacrificed his freedom for those things? He was not so sure.

His hand caressed the sleeping auk, slowly, tenderly, across the length of its body. The bird opened its dull eyes, which appeared deep having lost their reflection. It seemed to be giving him permission to look into them, to delve into its mind filled only with calm before an incomprehensible death the auk lay waiting for, unmoving, since panic was pointless. Whatever was meant to happen would happen.

Elinborg cut a fish into pieces and both of them pleaded with the bird, opening its beak and pushing the bits inside, massaging its neck to force them down. Worried, Gus settled down for the night next to his friend. Around four in the morning, Prosp made a noise—a cry, more like. Gus went straight over to sit on the ground near the basket. The auk's eye had turned brown again, the white had reappeared. Gus placed the basket between his bent legs and leaned against the wall. The auk slept, perhaps even dreamed. Gus wrapped his arms around it, careful not to squeeze Prosp too tight, and let his head fall against the bird's feathers, which emitted a smell of seaweed rot, and rubbed his cheek—or rather his beard—against the plumage.

He woke. Something hard was scratching his scalp, something resembling a flat stone, somewhat cold, or something pointy, tugging his hair stand by strand, not hard but enough to feel it. His head rested on his arm on the edge of the basket. He couldn't feel Prosp under him; he worried he'd crushed the auk. Gus turned and saw only a long neck, no head, moving against his temple. He realized Prosp was gently smoothing out his hair just as he had once smoothed Prosp's feathers, that Prosp was grooming him just as Gus had done when Prosp was moulting, possibly even delousing Gus, just as the bird would have deloused an auk friend.

THE GREAT AUK HAD BEEN SICK AND HAD GOTTEN better. It could have died, from a surfeit of emotion or bacteria, but had survived.

On the beach where Gus had gone walking alone at dusk during Prosp's convalescence, he tried to look out at the sea all the way to the horizon, to the farthest possible point. The desert, he believed, must look much like the sea; this void, or this place full of a matter not made for people, that cared not whether humans found it hospitable, pierced through him—almost literally, in fact, as if an arrow had struck him, as it would a rubber balloon, deflating his skin, letting it collapse to the ground, a poor thing turned useless.

In that moment, Gus felt lighter than pollen, insignificant but at the same time absolute. He knew he was part of the universe, much like the pebble to the right of his shoe, indistinguishable to him from another of its kind three yards away; from the faraway wave, which he was certain he could see forming again elsewhere, although that was surely another wave altogether; from the blade of grass on the hill, which blended in among the other blades of grass yet was undoubtedly itself unique. Suddenly, people had no more importance in that world, which breathed on its own and of its own accord, a world indifferent to his presence, which had existed before any human being had laid eyes on it and would continue to exist after. No more or no less importance than a wood shaving among millions of wood shavings. He was no longer anything, not anything with a name, corporeal form, a smell, habits, tastes, a morphing individuality. And strangely he felt freer, reassured to be of a kind with the wave, to lend company to the fly hovering over the black sand, and better able to converse, more minute, modest, and equal to all things, with an infinite universe that did not respond back.

So exhilarating was this feeling and so new that each day he came to seek it out again at the shore. Sometimes when the effect was spent, when instead of feeling a oneness and an unfamiliarity, he saw only the vaguely smudged line of the horizon, the lapping, the mechanics of the wind and swell instead of the stunning spirit of a wave, he would dig deep within himself to dredge up other mysterious reflections. He watched a gull dive and catch a fish in open water and wondered what the fish was thinking when it stopped breathing, in the instant when the bird's beak had already closed over its body. Did the fish realize it had been captured—it alone, out of hundreds of others? Had it considered its cruel luck? Or had it accepted its fate, since such was and had always been the way of things between fish and gulls?

In those moments, he would think of how his great auk, for some time now, had not crushed a fish in its beak in the wild. The bird was far from its kind and its home, and now a stranger to the sea, which before it would have crossed to perform, on the dry land of a lost little island, its reproductive duties. And the auk would have loved its young, absolutely, and known the companionship of other great auks with whom Prosp would have swum in the sea. If Prosp were to die, who other than Gus and Elinborg would remember it? Did the lingering memory belonging to two humans carry the same weight as that of the great auks? And if its species scarcened, what right did Gus have to keep Prosp from the others, if Prosp could help sustain it?

Just before Gus had departed for the Orkneys, Cuvier had published an article on the dodo bird, which had died out. It had to be admitted: There was a striking resemblance between Prosp and the seabird from Mauritius. Both had atrophied wings, shorn by good fortune, the two magnificent species had decided not to fly anymore since they had everything ahead of them, at the heart of gravity. And Gus feared that an omen lay therein.

But no, the dodo had to be an exception, an accident. Animals do not simply disappear—he interrupted the thought. Earth is nothing but abundance. It was true that the mammoth and the Megalonyx—an enormous sloth, as great as a mastodon—had long ago vanished. And it must be true, too, that creatures were transformed, smote by catastrophes or sometimes due to changing conditions, one species grew more adept and proliferated as another dwindled. But nature, so well-oiled, so balanced, impeded the end of creatures that were harmless to humans. And the earth was so vast that, perhaps, somewhere in the Pacific, or at the frozen poles, dwelled all the species thought to be dead.

And yet, that which diminishes can disappear entirely; it was only logical. Albeit unthinkable. When this idea came to him, Gus had the feeling of finding himself before a wall. Nothing on this earth, in this transcendent harmony, could be wiped out. Finally, it was because of this desert of a sea at sunset, because of the sickness Prosp had endured, that Gus began longing to send the auk back to its own kind, because each thing belonged to a world vaster than them—or simply because he wished the best for Prosp. At that time, he had been corresponding with Buchanan. The Scotsman spoke of settling down, maybe in Aberdeen, maybe in Edinburgh. His wife could not bear the isolation of the Orkneys any longer. But, for the most part, Prosp remained central to their correspondence, as well as Gus's profession, since Buchanan had read his work. He wrote to Gus the following letter:

Did you know that in 1816 white bears arrived in Iceland and devoured almost every fox and fallow deer? The poor Icelanders found themselves alone with the seals, I suppose. Prosp might be happy there, and perhaps your wife, who seems of an adventurous spirit and does not fear the isolation or cold of the place, might be happy there too. I could even visit, now that my family and I will be settling in the comfort of the city and all its distractions. I doubt they would miss me if I were away for a voyage of a few months.

I often travel for my work, you see. In Canada, I saw marvellous and horrendous things. The marvellous: a bison. I discovered the giraffe thanks to you, and there I discovered an enormous creature right next to me, three times the size of a cow maybe, with what I'd call a coat, or a fur stole behind its head and over its shoulders like an old woman at the opera. The horrendous: I watched an entire group of these magnificent beasts cross a river and swim, yes, swim and battle against the current with great difficulty, on land they are so strong; and then, just as they managed to, still shaken from the trek across, I watched the trappers I was with butcher them.

It seems common practice. But I did not expect the sight of all that blood and the pain and confusion of the animals these men finished off simply because they could to affect me so. Naturally, during all of this, I thought of Prosp. And hence the strange idea of Iceland where the bird might find contentment with a few others of its species, which you could protect, since what's the difference between one or ten, in the end?

Gus had no desire to go to Iceland, of course, nor to breed auks. That said, Buchanan wasn't wrong. Prosp had the right to live with other great auks and could even do its part to repopulate the species. He imagined his friend wrapping a wing around the neck of other auks backdropped by an idyllic landscape of waves and rocks, brown-tinged eggs shining against bellies and between their feet, and fish that, once swallowed, seemed to flow down their gullets.

The breeding grounds of great auks were far from endless in this part of the Atlantic. If he thought about it, there were few choices, and really, only one place still seemed worthwhile: the Saint Kilda archipelago. Eldey was now a mass grave. From time to time, the mariners told of sightings. At that thought, Gus saw the whole world correct course, as though the globe, thrown off for a moment by the dwindling of Prosp's species, were being set back to its rightful axis, the way it had always been seen. The chances of encountering other Prosps, while minute, were better than nothing. It seemed an interesting equation: everything or nothing.

PROSP'S SPOTS WERE ALREADY REAPPEARING IN APRIL 1837 when Gus boarded a boat belonging to Elinborg's brother, Signar. He would use the trip to St. Kilda to study the multitude of birds nesting there. Signar was quite excited, enthused at the idea of conducting such serious research in a place he had visited a hundred times without considering it could be of any importance. On the way, they dropped anchor near uninhabited islands, then spent two days in the Hebrides, near a port, hiding Prosp all the while for fear someone would think to steal the auk from them. Everywhere, they saw seals at rest, everywhere, puffins whirling in the water.

Every day on the boat, Prosp cried out in joy, neck craned toward the horizon, the ocean, the sea spray. The auk reached out its wings for the water to flow over its body. Gus had built it a fairly large wooden cage and nailed it to the deck. By day he walked the bird, attached to a cord that was tied to the cage. Prosp was sometimes very quiet, head always held high, waiting for the sea spray. Sometimes Gus felt envious of this element that had turned his seabird into a bewitched creature, impatient for each variation of light. He was getting acquainted with a new Prosp, a Prosp prey to instinct, brimming with an instant understanding of the phenomena all around, a Prosp no longer dependent on Gus, no longer watching for him or waiting for him in the mornings. The great auk before him seemed to know the reason for their voyage. It did not try to escape, and Gus soon realized there was little point in tying the bird up. Prosp was unafraid of the squalls or the waves that sometimes crashed over the deck. One day, taking Prosp in his arms, Gus noticed that even the auk's smell had changed, and the bird now gave off a reek of kelp with strong notes of dead fish.

The closer they drew to St. Kilda, the more Prosp's chest puffed out. The auk walked majestically about the deck, head pulled into its upper neck, beak serious, enormous and hooked, casting a proprietary gaze over the ocean. Signar and Gus joked about it, both relegated to mere ignorant sea-foam as Prosp threw them haughty looks and watched them battling with the sail, or cried out to alert them of a sudden gale or some manoeuvre deemed blunderous. However, near dawn, the auk would still call out to Gus, a feeble, sweet cry ending in a trill. Gus would take Prosp from the cage, sit next to the bird, and caress the feathered head already leaning against his shoulder. They would part ways at first light, leaving Prosp to once again strut about the deck.

The passing puffins made no impression on Prosp, and as for the seals, given the boat's protection, the auk did not seem to take any interest. It smoothed its feathers, fastidiously, several times a day. Gus thought this was the auk making itself handsome, true to its nature, ahead of meeting its own kind. Even Prosp's new scent of sea spray, fish, and seaweed must have been to win over its friends-to-be.

One day, they saw the St. Kilda archipelago in the distance. Gus took out a sketchbook on which he would draw the colony and a notebook to record his observations; with any luck, he'd witness at least one display of courtship. Great auks were said to mate for life, but Gus wondered if it were not, for Prosp, already too late.

He counted around a dozen birds, most perched on a ten-foot-tall rock. Gus was so excited, so engrossed in his mission that failing felt inconceivable. The cacophony of a million birds of all different species nesting on the cliffs grew deafening as they passed a cliff higher and steeper than any he had ever seen. At first, the noise made him think of sounds as loud as tolling church bells, then as they approached the shore farther on, it seemed more like a million small sleigh bells chiming all around them.

The great auks took up very little space on the beach, all the more so as they were very spread out, some resting just above the shoreline on a smallish rock. Gus stopped the boat twenty metres from shore and, for the first time, dropped his auk into the water without the cord. Strangely, Prosp, who had been calm and silent on the boat, now with a certain seriousness, or even reverence, entered the water.

Prosp floated like a duck, while no doubt studying the members of its species, fighting a purely natural sense of apprehension. Then Prosp dove down into the water, and Gus saw nothing more for ten minutes. He scanned the water, growing fearful. Prosp could not have swum off, could not have been eaten as there were no predators in sight. What did Gus know, though, of animal psychology, or shyness? Not much. Finally Prosp appeared under a wave crashing onto the beach, and stood up, stopped short, took another two steps, then stopped again. Gus recognized the bird at once. What other bird could it be but Prosp, his courageous Prosp? For once, the weather was wonderful. The sky was blue, the shapes on the beach perfectly visible. They did not move but all turned their heads toward the new arrival, Ulysses of great auks coming home to its own.

Prosp edged forward, beak lowered—to demonstrate peaceful intentions, thought Gus—and wobbling terribly, more than usual, from what must have been nerves. His great auk walked along the beach two, three metres from another auk, reaching its neck out, wings moving little, or rather, keeping stiller than ever. This other bird pretended not to notice Prosp, while the other great auks looked on from afar, appearing concerned with cleaning little things strewn about at their feet. Breeding season had yet to begin, the birds were building nests, some carrying pebbles in their beaks. Gus wondered whether Prosp should have brought an offering or two. But, again, what did Gus know of the customs of birds, in general, or of those of great auks in particular? Really, he was beginning to feel quite useless.

Gus was now just as nervous as Prosp. And just like Prosp, he was scared; even more, in fact, for at least Prosp was taking action. It was a new feeling. Never had Gus felt anything like it before, for anyone. Elinborg, his mother, his friends—none of them had ever been mistreated or rejected. Gus knew the pain of a bruised ego, to be sure, his own or his friends', but this was something everyone overcame. He had not worried for his mother when, for instance, she'd stayed angry at a cousin a whole year after being mocked for dressing like an old maid. And his mother had not fretted when Gus began secondary school—then again, he was long past the need for childish overprotection by that point and, in any case, would never have let on to the slightest perturbation in mood. But now, as the seabird he felt responsible for appeared weaker than these other, undeniably more hardened birds, Gus was shaking in his boat.

His auk stuck out its neck toward the strange bird in front of it. It was a modest and respectful gesture, yet at the same time daring. The reaction was immediate: a cry, a peck—but no bite—three steps forward, wings behind, Prosp quickly stepping back. The other great auks, farther down on the beach or perched on the rock, stopped what they were doing and watched the scene. Gus thought he heard Prosp emit a plaintive cry, but he must have imagined it; from where he was there was no way he could have heard it.

Prosp wobbled over to another creature and was met with the same greeting, the same rigorous choreography. Gus should have taken out his sketchbook, but with the tension in the air he didn't even think to. If things continued this way, he would never get back to the boat where Signar was awaiting him come nightfall. He was starting to get cold. An hour or so of daylight still remained.

Prosp was no longer moving, or approaching the other birds, just standing still on a bit of rocky ground near the water, but retained an expression, a kind of noble bearing, that brought Gus reassurance. One of the great auks waded out to swim, another followed, jumping off the rock. Gus studied them. What he saw was a group of auks coming together again after the long voyage across the sea. Birds were copulating on the shore; after a certain time went by and the scene played out repeatedly, Gus seemed to have gotten a clear sense that there were three established couples. For Prosp, this meant a few lone birds were left. Gus would have guessed three, but could have been wrong.

Prosp, perhaps for something to do, dove into the ocean as well, but did not go see Gus in his boat, nor swim far from the shore. Instead it floated and dipped its neck into the water like a swan, smoothing its tail and the feathers on its back. Then Prosp returned to the beach, riding the swell to be delivered to a rock. Dusk was nigh. Gus's eyes adjusted to the dim light. He would have to go back to the boat soon, leave Prosp to figure things out on the beach, to try to be up at dawn and get back as soon as possible to see Prosp. He left, anxious, but sure that he had done the right thing. That night he and Signar spoke very little. When his wife's brother asked for details of Prosp's progress, Gus only shrugged.

The next day at sunrise, Gus set foot for the first time on the island, choosing a spot at a distance from the auks yet close enough to study them. He took notes. Prosp seemed not to notice him and had not moved since Gus had left, remaining away from the others, at about the circumference of a circle about fifteen metres in diameter. Prosp was alone, seemingly invisible to the others. The great auks swam, they returned to the shore; Prosp swam, but only a little, before quickly returning to the beach.

Then Prosp tried to approach the other birds again, avoiding the couples, focusing on what Gus imagined to be the birds that had yet to mate. So different was Prosp's attitude, so unassured that there was no chance of Gus mistaking Prosp for one of the other great auks. When nothing was happening, Gus took notes on the gannets flying and nesting on the high cliffs, the northern fulmar that lived only in St. Kilda, gull-like in appearance but not of the same family. After about twenty minutes of observing things other than Prosp, he stopped and scanned the tiny colony of great auks again for the bird he knew.

Near noon, the birds began to stir. Even from a distance, there came a liveliness and gaiety; all the island was alive with excited cries, every inch of land and rock became a single agitated and chaotic dance honouring the sun that, even on St. Kilda, shone undeniably at its zenith. The island had not yet become a nursery. No birds had laid eggs, the celebration was mature, frenetic, punctuated with clashes, clips of the beak and declarations of love among birds of a kind. Gus felt like Gulliver, infiltrating an unknown society, envious of its freedom, joy, and severity. When he again looked at Prosp, he saw his auk shake its feathers, which at first stood on end then smoothed out into their habitual shiny tails. Then it spread its wings and ran toward another great auk, throwing its neck to the sky and singing, it seemed to Gus, though he could hear nothing amid the din. The other bird stretched out its wings and seemed to call back, no doubt warbling its own song.

From that moment, Gus's attention never wavered. The heaviness, the oppressive feeling he'd had since they arrived, was lifting. Prosp had come home to the other great auks and was beginning to be accepted among them. Great auks were marvellous creatures, Gus thought, allied and peaceful. Prosp took a quick step back to do something, clearly occupied by a new and intriguing thought, and came quickly back to the great auk who had sung back. Gus's auk had a pebble in its beak, which it dropped at its feet. So the mystery was solved: Prosp was a *he*, a male auk beginning his courtship and nest building.

Gus grabbed a bit of charcoal and started sketching what would be his final moments with Prosp. He didn't know whether he was happy to see Prosp return to the wild or sad to have to leave him. In the drawings, the sketch of Prosp was in close-up, a pebble in his bill, every small detail of his plumage entwined with that of the female auk, which he had sketched more roughly. And yet, from where Gus was standing, he could see neither Prosp's feathers nor his eyes, nor the pebble really either.

The sun clouded over more and more. Then there erupted a sudden panic among the auks: cries, two heads locked together by the beaks, which would appear to be locked in embrace if not for the furious beating of wings, striking the backs and sides of both birds with hundreds of slaps. Prosp, since he was one of the two, rolled on the ground, offering his chest to the other animal—perhaps the mate of the female Prosp had sought to woo—and the rival auk threw itself on Prosp, and Prosp, clever as he was, grabbed the bird's bill with his own to keep it from biting. But the other bird did not back down.

Something had sullied Prosp's right side, a mud-like smudge that could only have been blood. Gus leaped up, ready to run and protect his friend, even if he could only rally his champion, as he might cheer on a horse at the tracks. Yet he kept silent; he had no right to interfere: This was Prosp's education. Prosp rolled on the ground with the other auk. They both stood up again and eyed each other, beaks raised to the sky, as the female waddled over to the bird that was not Prosp and nuzzled its neck. The fight was over. Prosp had lost.

Time passed. Gus saw Prosp face down, curled up, feathers gashed, all alone at the other end of the beach. Gus thought perhaps Prosp might still find another mate, but he was unsure of the sex of the two remaining single birds. It was beginning to turn cold; from afar, Gus thought he saw Prosp shivering. The other auks were turned away from Prosp. It was raining. Prosp got to his feet, inched back toward the rock. His injuries must only have been surface wounds, as he was trying to stay upright, proud, all in all. He approached a couple of auks and was chased away, approached a single bird, his neck low to the ground, soft, long, so dexterous it seemed magical, poised to wrap around the other bird's neck, before making a timid gesture: humbly, sweetly offering his beak. The other auk kept still and let Prosp nuzzle its neck. A few seconds later, the bird jutted out its head, knocking against Prosp's, while its body hugged Prosp's and its wings beat at him—hundreds of blows where the wounds were still open. Then something happened that Gus hadn't been prepared for: This depleted colony, an aborted embryo of a vaster whole, which should have celebrated this newcomer's arrival, moved as one, a single beak made of many sharp beaks, against Gus's companion. The sounds of other birds on the island had dissipated. Night was about to fall and, amid the relative calm, as the other birds raised hue and cry, a saraband of mad witches screeched in terror behind Prosp, who, to escape them quicker or out of pure terror had slid right down the rock on his belly, useless legs flapping against the sky, stunned to find neither sea nor swell to carry him to safety.

Was it sorrow, or anguish, or shame an animal felt when bereft of friends and a future? Prosp wandered alone back to the beach, hunched over almost horizontal with his beak low. He climbed a rock, across from the spot where he had been chased off, then down on a ledge. It was low tide, near dusk. Prosp flattened himself against the rock ledge, or lay down, and stopped moving. The white spots on his head stood out against the black rock of the ledge, yet that head was limp and amorphous, his beak stuck into stone. His eyes must have been closed. The joyful creature Gus knew so well had disappeared, replaced by a bird made small, now crumpled on a tiny ledge, a bird no doubt unaware he was a great auk, a magnificent beast, the largest of all its penguin and auk relatives, the best swimmer of all birds, and perhaps the smartest of all animals in the northern hemisphere.

Gus, in his boat, approached, rowing as fast as he could to the shore. Prosp still wasn't moving, mineral as the rock he seemed ready to sink down into. No doubt he was dreaming of becoming a fossil, one of the many on this beach: fossils of old ferns, disappeared shells, worms dead for millions of years. Around him, Gus saw feathers fly like butterflies or insects, and when he was a dozen metres away, he could make out Prosp's bare skin, a patch where hundreds of plumes had been plucked. At four metres off, he thought he heard Prosp whimpering—but no, his bird was, in fact, quiet as ever. And at two metres away, Gus called to Prosp, but got no reaction.

Gus could no longer see his eyes, as the white spots around them faded into the night, and his body blended into the rocky relief.

The shallow, quiet water was as dark as viscous oil. Gus had to tie the boat and climb up to the ledge, all of three metres tall, but there was nothing to tie it to. He pushed the boat up against the rocks. He would have a minute, he wagered, to grab hold of Prosp and get back in before the current took hold. His foot slipped at first, then he found a cranny to push his toe into. Prosp lay at chest height. Gus quickly grabbed him, sliding his hands under Prosp's wings. Prosp made no sound or move to struggle. In the boat, Gus tended to Prosp, cleaning his wounds, and what felt like a bone moving beneath his thumb—vestige of a glory lost.

The loneliest animal in the world lay before him. An animal unlike any other. When he was with Gus and Elinborg, Prosp was the only one of his kind, an animal living among creatures with no common language, no longer really a great auk but an ersatz, half auk and half duck, since he led the life of a duck, in essence, penned up or floating on the water's surface instead of exploring the ocean's depths.

Yet—and here was Prosp's good nature—Prosp recovered from his wounds, inner ones included. He was a great auk that would be the last of his line, rejected by his kind, a forever-lost Ulysses who would never stop circling Ithaca, who did not want to die. Maybe he knew love, maybe he loved Gus and Elinborg and the sheep that sometimes wandered over to his pen, intrigued, with whom it always looked as if Prosp were speaking from the other side of the fence. After the voyage, Prosp never once fell ill again. Sometimes Elinborg would let him into the house. With his air of a troubled mind, Prosp seemed almost human. And so this creature, unique in all creation, who would never teach his young to swim or eat from the beak of another auk, had a destiny unlike all others: the destiny of a hero, a survivor, living a life no other great auk would ever know.

WHEN HE RETURNED FROM ST. KILDA, ELINBORG found her husband distracted, though perhaps, she reflected, she was confusing distraction with obsession, to which he was indeed prone. Gus worked long hours, shuttered in his study, and, at dinner or on their walks, he seemed always to be thinking of something other than what they were doing.

"You wouldn't even notice if I up and disappeared one day, just like that, right in front of your nose," she told him, then darted off up the hill.

He ran after her, grabbed hold of her, and threw her over his shoulder, burying his face as her flying, tangled hair tickled his neck and chin. He pretended to swallow her locks, to be strangled in her hair, then they fell to the ground and rolled down the hill. After, he apologized for being so lost in his thoughts. Something on St. Kilda had deeply troubled him.

He kept circling an idea, but couldn't quite pin it down. He told her the story of Mary Shelley's *Frankenstein*, which she had not read. He was not about to create a new person, he told her, but he shared the mad scientist's obsession for something truly tremendous, as tremendous as humanity itself, maybe even as the creation of the world. She began calling him Frankenstein, and referring to his "laboratory" when he did not want to leave the study.

At a table by the window, he watched Prosp a ways off in his pen and wondered if he shouldn't try to find Prosp a better companion than the sheep that came and went, and sometimes abandoned Prosp altogether. He scribbled down sentences, crossed them out, rewrote them. Batches of memories surfaced, and he tried to order them: Buchanan, in Stromness, telling him about the black market, Jakupsson talking of witches—the great auks they took for witches and slaughtered. He felt his brain stop working as it reached what seemed like a cliff, but instead it turned out to be something blue, nearly placid, but truly uncanny.

So, once again, he looked up from the page. He saw birds in the sky; the sea, where he thought he could make out dolphins coming up from the waves for a second before diving back again; gulls catching the smaller fish as they flew over the water; and on the hills to the left, thousands of field mice devouring thousands of invertebrates—a world of abundance, where every creature ate some other, yet all survived. His thoughts then turned to hunting, of the pheasants that were killed while their species persevered.

There was something Gus couldn't quite grasp, but what? He could feel his mind stutter then stop, and then he'd lean back over the page. That which was alive could not disappear. Of course, there had been Cuvier's theory of catastrophism, which explained the extinction of species long lost, enormous creatures like the mastodon and the Megalonyx, whose traces had been discovered. And of course, Gus, along with the rest of his generation, had cast aside this theory, preferring Lamarck's hypothesis that a species only changed over time, becoming the modern version everyone knew. Gus's generation also knew humans had coexisted with the mastodon; and since humans were the last species to appear, there could not have been a catastrophe in which everything had gone extinct without exception—*Homo sapiens* and mastodons both.

The whole thing was confused. Humans destroyed other species, species that were *detrimental*, although the small rodents somehow managed to survive. Everyone knew this, and here again Gus found himself hitting a wall, again, his brain faltered and shrivelled. He was missing some element that might have ordered his thinking, forged a logic from all these scattered, unconnected ideas, without shedding light on his situation—that of Prosp, who could in no way be considered *detrimental.*

He wrote to the naturalists and paleontologists he knew, to Garnier, of course, who responded:

> *Without a doubt the great auk populations are diminishing, that much is known. Your worrying may be exaggerated, though. Is it really justified? Might not they have hidden away somewhere? One day they'll reappear, more numerous than ever.*

Gus was more or less of the same opinion. What's more, had the great auk colonies not deserted the Canadian coasts, chased off by the mass arrival of cod fishers? And what had those colonies done? They had rebuilt here, a place they knew already but had underexploited up till then. All to say, if they had relocated once, they could do so again.

Kroyer, who he had met in Copenhagen, shed even more light on the subject:

> *Have you read Charles Lyell? His theory is what has happened before is still happening, or rather what we're facing has already been. Which means that, since the enormous, monstrous species we've found the bones of have gone extinct, it follows that other species can, too. The world is in constant motion, progressing, in such a regular, slow manner we cannot see the changes. Cuvier's catastrophes, that abrupt change, the sudden reforming of a new world, are, I hope,*

behind us once and for all. The idea is more one of cycles. So perhaps one day we'll see a mammoth reappear, which would be amusing, though not for elephants, I fear. A joke, of course, but I sometimes like to dream it could happen.

Gus procured himself the English edition of Lyell, since no French was available. What a powerful, prodigious work, such novel ideas. The subtitle of *Principles of Geology* said it all: *Being an attempt to explain the former changes of the earth's surface, by reference to causes now in operation.* As for other species, Lyell could see different explanations for their extinction: changes to their habitations (and here Lamarck, with his beliefs in happy adaptation or, in fact, amelioration, appeared truly outdated); competition with another species; and humans, who disposed of detrimental animals, as usual, but whose growing population led to the reduction, or even destruction, of certain animal populations. And here he spoke of the emu, which he believed to be at risk. The process, in reality, did not much bother Lyell, for he considered it a natural response to the laws of nature. It was as unavoidable as death, against which there was no point struggling. In a sense, it was life, was a way Gus could think of it, and this idea gave the whole a pessimistic, resigned, and brutal cast.

When he replied to Kroyer's letter, he told him of his own problem: "None of Lyell's mechanisms of extinction apply specifically to great auks. Not climate, since its habitat has not changed, and less than thirty years ago, within the same geographic area, they were abundant. Nor competition between animals, since I dare say the great auk has no enemies, that neither seals nor puffins need to claim its territory or defeat it. Which leaves humans: But how can great auks, who live far from us, be detrimental? I cannot see it. So can it be that we, as humans, have made a mistake?"

As he finished his letter, Gus felt as though he understood the nature of the wall in front of him: The injustice endured by the great auk could not be comprehended, since the very essence of the injustice was inexplicable.

Dargenais, a friend of Gus's and an amateur naturalist, had written to him about John Fleming, whom Gus had distractedly read before he'd left France.

> *He explains,* wrote Dargenais, *that the progress of human societies, and I'm citing from memory here, influence the geographic distribution of animals. Many species in England have disappeared—the beaver, for instance, is gone but is not, in fact, dead. This shows how humans can have devastating effects on animal species, but that our power, I imagine, remains somewhat limited with regard to the immense surface area of the world.*
>
> *You would like Fleming (an influence on Lyell). I think he also had some story with a great auk that he wanted to bring home. And it died in the end. Apparently it affected him deeply. I have no idea if it's true. In closing, I can't think of a recently extinct species, with the possible exception of the dodo bird, but the date of that is unknown; and it lived on land, bound to an island. Not knowing how to swim, or fly, it could not flee when predators arrived. Which is not the case for Prosp.*

Gus could not plausibly deny that the "immense surface area of the world" was a fact; so, yes, no doubt somewhere there must be other great auks tucked away. If a species could have once travelled, it could do so again, why would that be so difficult to believe? In Iceland in 1816, the bear had eradicated the fallow deer, yet fallow deer still existed elsewhere, and now, thanks to Dargenais, he was reminded of this story of beavers and the English, for wasn't America now teeming with them? So, following Lyell's reasoning: What had been once can be again, had to be again, and great auks could be multiplying in a corner of the globe unknown to him.

Elinborg fell pregnant. It was a time when she had been growing closer to Prosp. She was usually the one who walked Prosp along the beach for his swim. To her great surprise and Gus's, too, Prosp no longer needed to be tied to a cord. The time on Saint Kilda had changed him as well. Gus felt that the auk no longer desired to live in the wild, where he perhaps no longer had his place. He swam out farther than ever now, and he always came back.

A girl was born, and they named her Augustine, after her father, and because, to Elinborg's ears, French names had a deliciously exotic ring. Gus started travelling again. He went to Iceland with an expedition that had stopped over on the Faroe Islands. He travelled through the fishing villages of Reykjavik. The island's inhabitants lived in houses covered in green grass—this did not surprise him, he had already seen many like them in those parts.

He collected plant specimens and helped conduct hydrographic surveys. The year before, on a different expedition, he had visited Greenland and seen the icebergs there. Never had he imagined something so beautiful. But they were also somehow an exact representation of that wall blocking his thinking, its material form, immense and blue, smooth and terrifying. The scene before him appeared so stupefying that for an instant he told himself he could die right there, crushed by its splendour. He was immobilized by vertigo, unsteady on the ship's deck. And at the same time, it felt like he was flying.

On the way back, in northern Scandinavia, he took notes on the language of Lapland and on local medicinal decoctions, and carried out topographical surveys. He had a pair of reindeer-hide boots made, which he and Elinborg would realize, when he returned to the Faroes, were as tall as Augustine. Because the boots were supple and the fur inside soft, the child played with them as a toy. And they let her have them. Elinborg became pregnant again, and this time they chose the Faroese name Ottarr, in honour of the islands that had brought Gus such happiness, and because he was susceptible to the exoticism of Nordic words.

Prosp was not jealous of the children, although he did not like to be near them. He kept an eye on them, nonetheless, partially because he was distrustful of them. If one of them fell or banged themselves on something and Elinborg was not nearby, he would begin to screech until she returned. As soon as she did, he would waddle off with an air of slight disgust, his beak perfectly straight, no doubt feeling an obligation had been fulfilled and perhaps some slight compassion for this mother who, without him, would be quite lost. Gus wondered how Prosp could tell the difference between children and adults—how he could know these small humans to be fragile and helpless and in need of assistance and saving.

One day, Gus found a goose at the market in Tórshavn and bought it. It was somewhat scrawny, with a typical goose-like surliness, but its size, close to Prosp's, made him hope that it might be of interest to the auk, so it could keep him company. If the two of them fought, they could always cook the goose up and eat it. He and Elinborg watched them stand face to face in the pen—a true disaster. Prosp charged the goose, the feathers on his head upraised in anger and indignation. The goose started running, wings spread wide, and in a much more elegant manner than Prosp, it had to be said. The goose could lap Prosp, too, and managed to do so twice as it ran around the pen in utter distress, while Prosp was finishing a first circuit. The auk's sharp, loud cry, however, was much more frightening than the unfortunate fowl's.

Elinborg and Gus raced after the birds to prevent the carnage sure to come. Elinborg managed to catch the goose, blocking its neck with her arm. Gus caught a pecking from Prosp, who had gripped on to his earlobe. They removed the goose. When they closed the gate, Prosp wore his sulking expression, standing up straight over his feet, shooting daggers, or literal flashes of light, for Prosp knew how to play with the light's reflection, giving his eyes a dark glimmer.

They separated the birds for a few days, placing the goose on the other side of the pen. At first, Prosp pretended not to notice it, but soon Elinborg saw that the slightest movement of the goose and Prosp was alert, still outraged, but also curious. He would instantly stop eating, scratching, dunking his head in the water as soon as the goose came into his line of vision. A few days went by, and, just like with the sheep, Prosp began to go up to the barrier and look at the goose without his habitual hostility. As for the goose, it kept its distance, seeming to strut a few metres away, with an air of cruel indifference. Elinborg thought the goose to be playing a game, and Prosp acquiesced with a sigh; in other words, they were growing accustomed to one another's presence. One day, at last, arriving near the pen, Gus saw the two of them close together, their beaks touching on either side of the fence. The next day, they put them back in the pen together.

From then onward, the two birds often slept side by side, their necks enlaced. The goose's neck, longer than Prosp's, managed to wrap nearly all the way around his. They looked almost like an antique amphora, their black and white plumage standing out against each other. At night they sheltered beside each other in the barn, groomed each other's feathers.

They were inseparable most of the time, except when they ate, on either side of the barrier—one, grain; one, fish—or when Prosp went swimming.

Ottarr was three, Augustine close to five when, in 1843, Buchanan arrived on the Faroe Islands. He'd made a fortune in the fur trade and was now working for the Hudson's Bay Company. He was on his way to Canada. He had not changed, or even aged, by Gus's reckoning. He was just as pale as before, as tall and lanky; everything about him evoked a ribbon of seaweed with light brown hues, seaweed wavering in the water, supple, neither pretty nor ugly, strange.

They decided to set out on an excursion. The landscape was monotonous, most of all empty, the grass looked burned or reddened, at least, which made sense since it was October. They slept in a tent, by the campfire. In the distance they saw foxes, and the rabbits they were hunting. The cold air stung their faces, turning even Buchanan's face red. They talked as they walked. The static landscape, the feeling of being the only ones on the deserted stretch of land, majestic with what seemed like an endless row of hills, helped them focus. Buchanan told Gus he had not seen a single great auk on St. Kilda that year, without a doubt they had all been killed. Gus felt as though he were learning of the death of a personal enemy. For a moment, he felt a sigh of revenge, as though he'd had an old vendetta, a gale of satisfaction at seeing justice served. Then, just after, a tightness in his chest.

"I don't believe it," said Gus to Buchanan, adding the sound of a chord grinding against an anvil to each syllable, "it's impossible. They must have gone somewhere. Thirty, forty years ago, they were everywhere."

"You know about the ibex? In Savoie they were on the brink of extinction. The king of Piedmont-Sardinia decreed a moratorium on hunting a few years ago. So how is it impossible to think Man could destroy a species? Or save it? Tell me."

"But so quickly? No, I don't understand how. Look at the foxes over there."

And Gus motioned to a vague shadow in the distance leaping away. It might not have been a fox, but it didn't much matter.

"We won't eat them."

"The rabbits then, look, there!"

"How many babies does a rabbit have...? How many eggs for a couple of penguins or great auks? It's an easy calculation to make. Maybe our bird is no longer adapted to the world as it is now. Only an elephant has such paltry offspring."

Gus remembered the annual grindadráp here on the islands, he had gone one year. They herded the dolphins into the bay, then closed in on them, and the men left the shores and waded into the sea up to their knees, reeling them in with hooks, and ropes, onto the rocks where they slashed them open and broke their spinal cords. The blood drenched their clothes, the ground. At first, Gus hadn't been shocked. The disgust came later, when he saw dolphins cut apart while still half-alive, or watched as a mallet came down on an animal's ribs. At the end, they shared the meat and blubber among themselves, food that would see the islanders, who were poor, through the months to come. Gus and Elinborg had taken some too.

Gus remembered men like these, at the grindadráp, back on Eldey, smashing auk eggs. Men who likely, back home, partook in similar fishing rituals, just with different names. And he thought of the people he knew, friends and relations, who pulled tufts of wool from the sheep with their bare hands. And yet, he emphasized to Buchanan, the dolphins lived on, the sheep had not committed suicide.

"Not so for the great auks of St. Kilda," said Buchanan.

"But what if they've gone to the Antarctic Ocean or the Indian Ocean? Why not? What about the penguins? Where there are penguins, wouldn't they find great auks? Frankly, don't you find them quite similar? Don't you think Prosp would be happy at the Cape of Good Hope?"

"He won't be happy anywhere without you, ever again. Think about it, Auguste. All things rare are bound to disappear, it's Malthus, it's exponential. Humankind prospers and multiplies infinitely, like an upside-down pyramid. And that which diminishes reduces much in the same way, very quickly. It's a matter of *logic*. Sorry to say it, but no one has spotted any great auks in the Cape."

Gus bit into a cold sausage as he sat there on the coarse grass next to his friend. Everything before them—the landscape, the entire earth—seemed immutable, nothing seemed to have ever changed or to need to change one day. He did what generations before him had done here: walked, fished, watched the death of a whale, or the puffins and fulmars nest on the cliffs. The damp and the mould returned every year in their house after being eradicated. So why would a bird not come back?

He wanted to hold tight to Garnier's optimism: nothing changes for good, vital forces are at play, and life always reforms anew. But he didn't know what to say. To be sure, once numbers fall below a certain level they can only keep falling, and an animal that lays but one egg a year, while the general population dwindles, can no longer ensure the same reproduction of the species.

If a hundred great auk couples produce one hundred eggs, and, say, forty of their young die before adulthood, twenty die in various accidents, that leaves forty auks to experience the same proportions of loss, since the external conditions are identical, and thus all end up gone—perhaps everything was disappearing, without him even noticing, and while Gus chewed his bite of meat, the world was shifting, slowly, without him feeling the ground move, the earthquake from under his feet. So yes, at that moment everything was already different, sad and morbid, brutal and senseless, everything bloodstained in the end.

They went home to Gus and Elinborg's. Buchanan would leave the next day at first light. In the evening, the three of them paid Prosp and the goose a visit. The auk approached Buchanan and pinched his pant leg in his beak, then stared at him for several seconds. Buchanan felt certain Prosp recognized him. He was touched and flattered. Gus said nothing, for in truth Prosp often showed a healthy curiosity toward any stranger, which only further demonstrated how Prosp was no longer a wild animal. It was as though Gus had created a new species: the domestic auk.

And, in truth, he saw no use for such a species. Prosp and his kin laid a single egg each year—not enough to feed a family. And they reproduced too slowly for them to be raised for meat. They were pretty birds, perhaps, but not beautiful like peacocks; Gus had trouble imagining what they could bring to a botanical garden. He felt uneasy; like Frankenstein, he had created a creature that would be alone forever, terrifying his companies, misunderstood by people and their pets—except for the goose, who, upon further reflection, had no other option save the roasting spit.

A WEEK AFTER BUCHANAN'S DEPARTURE CAME THE smell of whale blubber and Gus's first bouts of nausea, a reaction that, on the Faroes, presented a serious problem. And when his brother-in-law, Signar, coming back from the hunt, offered Elinborg a puffin to cook up, Gus locked himself in his study for twenty-four hours, refusing to speak to anyone. What was she thinking? How could his wife have been so stupid as to accept the corpse of a bird from the penguin family? Gus would have to sustain himself on cod alone, from then on. Everything around him reeked of fish. The salt, he was certain, was eating away at his bones and hair, strands breaking between his fingers. It was perfuming his cracked lips and toughened skin, stiffening his clothing, his entire person.

He dreamed of a place without fish, of the smell of the earth, or anything unsalted. Sometimes he thought of the south of France, the purple of lavender blooms, living rooms with vases of roses and peonies. He felt nostalgic for the trees, the forests, the flat and unmoving grasslands in place of the unstable, ever-shifting expanse of sea. He was sure his once-brown eyes had become washed out and taken on the pale, brackish hue of Buchanan's.

He could not help it, but he was suspicious of everyone. He was not afraid, not for himself or Elinborg, nor for the children, but he felt the brutality was bound to rub off on them. Instead of hands, he imagined he saw hooks, tufts of sheep wool pink with blood, or the head of a penguin. Barbarians, he thought, uncivilized, like this whole region, as the monotone fauna and grey landscapes, the imperfect white tones like cracked enamel—nothing bright, or radiant, or easy, no joyful yellow of a tit bird or comical squirrel coiffures. Only all that was harsh, adapted for survival alone; everything sad, or useful.

The more he thought about it, the less he wanted to keep the children there. He'd always imagined sending them to study in Denmark or France when they were older, but his thinking had been wrong: they had to leave now, while they were still young, leave the putrefied atmosphere, a life spent believing the sky was a grey cover and that they were the only living things between it and the ground under their feet, or that other than the roof of the barn or the house, no shelter from the rain, or from the gaze of neighbours, existed—and even then, the truth was that so few people lived there.

He spoke to Elinborg. She was neither for nor against it. She could not go to France, since she spoke no French. Perhaps Denmark? She did not think she would like living in Copenhagen, and yet, the thought of something new excited her. She did not understand, though, this obsession of her husband's for trees, his refusal to eat mutton, and his carrying on about colours and flowers. She was familiar with the beauty of gardens; she had seen it as a young girl, on the continent. She could not say whether it was something she missed.

Gus began shutting himself away more and more. In the morning, he had trouble getting up. As soon as he looked out the window, he wanted to go back to bed. One day, he feigned sick, and Elinborg made him stay in bed for a week, as she did with Ottarr or Augustine.

The only thing that still invigorated Gus was caring for Prosp in his pen. It looked as though they were plotting something: facing one another, they would remain still, just staring at each other. Gus lowered his head toward Prosp for minutes at a time, as though whispering; the two of them seemed crazed, fenced in the pen. Even the goose seemed exasperated. Why, Gus wondered, did he see in Prosp something indistinct and bigger than Prosp which weighed on his heart? Prosp couldn't even bring himself to have fun anymore. To see him stagger around, hiding when a bird of prey crossed the sky, only made Gus sad, as though the auk were merely a manifestation of a void, as though everything about him represented a paradox: the presence of a lack.

Gus blinked, and nodded his head to shake the image, but it kept coming back. And Elinborg, seeing his head swaying, his grimaces, started to worry about her strange husband. He, too, was frightened by his melancholy. It clung to him, spoiled the children's laughter, Elinborg's tender touch, the pleasure of work, and of sleep, which he overindulged in. The hours dragged. In the evening he waited for day, and by day he dreamed of the night, always aghast and disappointed by what came next. Without meaning to, his thoughts led to the idea of the end, for Prosp, of course, but Augustine and Ottarr as well. When the children ran up the hill, Gus imagined them running toward a precipice.

He no longer knew if he thought the place would turn them cruel or whether he felt the fragility of all things, imagining their inevitable aging, the hurt that could be inflicted on them one day and that one day they themselves might inflict. It felt, for Gus, like spending his life behind a curtain of rain—which was the reality, in fact—or behind a smudged pane of glass through which the rays of light shone, dulled by accumulated dust—which was not the case.

"Think on it, Auguste," Buchanan had said, "there aren't any great auks in Cape Town." He kept hearing this in his ear, and "that which is rare disappears." But how does someone disappear? What had he seen disappear in his life? His mother, when he was little, had managed to eliminate an ant colony in their home. And no doubt being attacked, and reduced, had meant reaching a turning point beyond which the colony was no longer viable, and the ants had disappeared.

It started out as a rumour, circulating for fifteen days: There were no more great auks on Eldey. Then the rumour got more detailed: The last two great auks on the island had been killed. Then Gus heard the whole story from a naturalist returning from Iceland, headed to the Orkney Islands. He'd met a sailor, recruited a month before by a merchant peddling marine curiosities to museums and collectors. The sailor had recounted to the naturalist how, on June 3, 1844, a month prior to Gus learning of this conversation, three men he was sailing with had landed on Eldey, where they'd noticed two birds on the shore. When they'd come back to the boat, two of them bore a strangled bird. Gus had no need to hear the details. He had seen it all before.

"And was there an egg?" he had asked his colleague.

"If there was, they left it behind."

When Gus went to see Prosp the next morning, he realized he was no longer looking at his auk but at a unique specimen, a fossil soon to be encrusted in a rock near the sea. He thought of the breeding couple that would leave a hole at the place they had occupied on this earth, a loss which might go unnoticed at first, but the fact of it would inevitably have consequences on the density of the maritime population: the fish they had devoured, the seaweed they had swum among.

And really, the balance must already have been upset, there must have been storms, lightning, a horde of witches descending on those gloomy islands where everything died at human hands. But no, that was not so. Dusk would have come as it did every day in summer, a little later each night, the light no doubt more orange than ordinary, the sea calmer than in days before, a deceptive calm in this place that knew only the cold, the raging winds, the perpetual damp of the sea spray. Nothing had happened except that two birds had, it seemed, been separated as they ran in their proud and inept manner across the shore when the mariners disembarked.

What if one of them should have escaped? Would it have returned to cover its egg and protect its offspring? And to what end? What had their last voyage across the ocean been like? Had they swum alone, or already side by side? They'd escaped orca and fin whales, walruses, then arrived on the cold, hard skerry to die.

Gus had Prosp between his knees and had not even noticed. He was petting him, without feeling Prosp's warm pulse beneath his fingers, or else he was noticing something other than the tight, fine feathers of the great auk he so loved, a bird that, if he died, would leave with the memory of a whole species, little known to Prosp, and that of the watery underworld, seldom explored by him.

Something else kept haunting Gus, and he dared not completely formulate the thought. It ached of regret, some foolish whim now irremediable: like Jules Dumont d'Urville boarding, for some ordinary journey, a train that derails, and dying in Meudon having only just discovered Adélie Land. Was it really so different from what Gus had done? Yet, being human, he was responsible. How could he put it? He would have been better able to stomach the great auk's disappearance could he have blamed a volcano, or orcas, or polar bears. But this seabird was dying off as it was used in stews, charred slabs of meat, oil no better than whale oil.

What did Gus see when he looked down at Prosp wedged between his knees, staring intently into the bird's serious brown eye? He could not think it yet: that once Prosp was gone, he would never again on this earth see that same deep gaze again, its dullness, the opaque membrane roll vertically to protect that iris, that pupil. The fact was he was afraid, and he dared not formulate such an obscene idea. After Prosp, no other such eye would ever look at him, since Prosp was not a horse whose traits could be found in another horse. After Prosp, no other bird would have the same characteristics of his extinct species.

Once again Gus wondered what his bird was thinking and whether he had the same anxieties. Perhaps Prosp, too, felt something was askew in the universe, like an eraser had begun to rub out his tail, his beak. It must have been strange to be Prosp, to have had to learn to live this way, to have had Gus as a friend, a creature that did not speak his language or with whom he would not swim in the ocean nor mate. Gus had the feeling suddenly of becoming a great auk, of thinking, of feeling the things Prosp felt, while the world, their world, gradually faded before them, and there together their hearts grew numb in the midst of a landscape slowly being drained of colour.

III

THEY NO LONGER SMELLED FISH IN THE AIR, THE salt no longer cracked Gus's skin, the wind no longer tangled Elinborg's hair, since now she brushed it straight over her ears and held it in place with a headband. A tutor saw to the children's education and brought them out once in a while to walk under the trees. They all liked Denmark: the wide streets, the sound of the horses on the paving stones, the crowds.

In 1845, Gus found a position at the University of Copenhagen. He had expanded his research to the flora of the north, and to biology. Several evenings a week, students came for supper at the house. They talked of many things, seriously, in a relaxed and simple familial setting. Their smallish house just outside Copenhagen had a wild garden and, of course, a swimming hole. It overlooked the sea, which was important for Prosp too. Boats passed by often, but the auk had grown used to them.

Prosp's life had changed little, save that, for the last month, he had been posing for a portrait with Augustine. It had been the painter's idea, and the girl's. It would make for a lovely portrait of the child—the severe, dangerous-looking beak of the bird against the little girl's simple cotton dress as she stared in the painter's direction or at the easel with a serious yet mischievous air, conscious as she was of posing. The background was water-lily green. For a stranger, the pairing of the bird, who was beginning to look more and more like a pastor, and the child, her braid a tad dishevelled, as though she'd been playing, appeared odd, but Gus felt that to their family it spoke to friendship, and the normalcy of life with Prosp.

Gus wanted to stop thinking about the future of great auks. His own bird was simply an unusual pet, a mark of eccentricity highly appreciated by his students and, of course, his comrade. There was no solution to the species' extinction, an event so serious, so colossal, that it was better not to think of it, and to be happy just to live. It was the precise reason he had pivoted his focus to flora. Losing a daisy seemed to him less devastating than the end of a living being, one with a voice and the ability to feel things.

Sometimes he thought of how in a few years' time someone might see the portrait of Augustine and Prosp and wonder what the chimeric creature pictured was, some sort of enormous guillemot with stubby wings and a bill like a rhino's horn. He entertained this thought while watching his bird and put it out of his head, since it provoked a sense of impotence, a vague guilt at not having known to catch other great auks on Eldey when he had saved Prosp, so he could protect them.

Prosp was aging, yet, surprisingly, still energetic and childlike. He adored crustaceans and preferred them to fish. Sometimes he would complain if they gave him herring too often. One day, he snatched a slice of bread Ottarr had left in the garden. And from then on, whenever someone had bread or a cookie in their hand, he sought to claim it by shamelessly screeching, shamelessly unafraid of a scolding. According to Gus, Prosp's incubated existence, never having to fight to eat, had led him to develop a capricious nature, one that was overly demanding, a little as though he considered himself equal to the children, whose parents were strict at times but surrendered more often than not.

And yet, alone with Prosp in the evening after his students

left, in the greenhouse he had built, Gus noticed his bird betrayed signs of melancholy. Except, he told himself, it was perhaps his own melancholy projected onto this animal staring into nothing, with a transfixed and foggy gaze. Gus would call him, motioning, and the bird would limp over, stretch out his neck for Gus to caress. As he had on the Orkneys, and even more so on the Faroes, Gus would pour three jugs of water onto his plumage. Prosp would straighten up, spread his stumped wings, and smooth his feathers under the impromptu cascade.

Gus was taking notes again, but notes of another nature, as though he were preparing an encyclopedia on the species that would advance knowledge far beyond the question of the auk itself. It began while wondering whether Prosp could still defend himself in the wild. Gus thought that instead, familiar with humans and confident, he would throw himself at the feet of the first mariner he saw for help, should danger strike. What, in the end, did Prosp know of his environment? He did not know he was a great auk, or that Gus and his kin were humans. He did not know that they *spoke*, uttering words with a specific meaning, or that when combined with other words this meaning could change. Their voices must have seemed to Prosp a humming evoking mood or intention: good humour alone when he waved at them in the morning, and good humour married with the intention of pleasing him when they brought Prosp some halibut for lunch, crying, "Here, Prosp, here."

For Prosp, everything must be natural, nothing strange, or perhaps strangeness was the intersection of all things. To put it another way: Not everything Prosp encountered had to be questioned. Knowing the use for a fork, a ladder, or a chair was of little importance. The fork was dangerous and useless, the ladder amusing for five minutes to stick your head through the steps, the armchair could serve as a promontory if you could make it up there in one jump—which Prosp had managed once or twice in his lifetime, at the cost of considerable effort.

Calling into question his surroundings would have been as vain as wondering why orcas had teeth. After all, great auks had accepted that horrid reality for centuries now; if it came to pass, they would die in the orca's jaw without a fight, no tears, no flash of reflection. Too bad, what an unlucky day. They did not want to die. But it was the risk, the end of the life of every auk, to end up eaten, just as auks ate krill. Suddenly, Gus realized he had never heard of an auk, great or small—or for that matter of a single fish—that had died of old age. No doubt older, feebler animals were devoured by predators; this was law, and none grieved friends or travel companions, or parents that disappeared into the belly of a whale.

Gus and Prosp both thought they were observing the same things, but Gus knew this was not, in fact, the case. For Gus, everything around them obeyed its own logic, but for Prosp everything came out of nowhere, the human in front of him, who walked, put on or took off a jacket or a hat, made absolutely no sense. The hat itself meant nothing—once placed on the table, no doubt Prosp made no more connection between the hat and hair or a head. Everything was absurd, and yet Prosp adapted, or rather he would never think to doubt what existed.

When Prosp posed with Augustine, he did not understand why he was asked to stay in one place for so long, near immobile—which was implausible—but in a small space, on a table, in profile. Of course, they could manage no more than five minutes, during which time the painter would whip off some sketches. On those occasions another side of Prosp came out: his gentleness, as he complied with an activity that even Augustine found tiresome, submitting because he wanted, it seemed, to make the little girl happy, to be with her at her request.

When he left the tabletop after crying to be put on the floor, he did not run out of the room, but moved to a corner, and just as the painter did, he watched the child standing there, as though lending encouragement to her endeavour. And in this there was a kind of modesty, a respect for codes he could not comprehend, something tender, a desire to partake in the shared life of this family which was, after all, his own.

There remained, however, a matter of some delicacy: Prosp had always given off a pungent smell, of fish but also a mustiness—a strong odour of fish, stagnating but not rotting. The auk had a keen sense of smell of his own and hated all artificial perfumes (upon smelling them he would turn away, as though embarrassed for their wearer). He could hunt down a crustacean anywhere: in the cupboard, on the second floor, buried underground, in the yard—Gus had tested this. He also loved, it had to be said, all natural bodily odours.

As for Gus, he had a poor sense of smell. And so, in this respect, he and Prosp lived in two very different worlds. It was Gus's vision that allowed him to understand a space or location without having to sniff anything. The world around him and even in nature felt lively and expressed itself in the past, present, and sometimes future, blending kilometres of knowledge that, in mere moments, came together in his mind. For Prosp, the world was an assemblage of different materials, whether dangerous or not, which no doubt came to him in a gradual way as he moved about a space. And, of course, if Gus were to swim in the ocean with Prosp, their situations would be reversed.

And yet, the two got along well. They trusted one another. There was a sort of intersection of two worlds, a crossover zone where they lived in harmony. Gus would have liked to say it was a space formed out of affection, but he knew this was false, that the space they inhabited had nourished their affection and not the opposite. They shared certain sensations: They understood one another as soon as their needs were at stake, when one of them was hungry, the pleasure of eating something good, thirst, joy at its relief, the effect of a caress or of a blow. Both had the same frame of reference and transposed their own experience onto the other. Their bodies felt the same way, and when either was tired they both closed their eyes.

Yet, outside that intersection, everything differed. Gus wondered which of them saw the world as it really was, in their own way; in truth, they both saw it for what it was. Prosp, for instance, seemed unable to distinguish certain colours. He was attracted to plants, with a noted preference for anything green or purple, even some of Elinborg's dresses—Elinborg, who, since they had moved to Denmark, wore a more varied palette of colour. But Prosp was indifferent to anything pale, pastel, grey, or brown; sometimes he seemed not to even notice a cloth fallen to the floor, tripping on it after. But perhaps Gus did not see every colour around him either, given that the world around them was nothing like the description the two might have created together if Prosp could speak. Gus thought the grass was green, but perhaps it had no colour at all. It could well be that auks and men lived by a series of conventions that kept them from measuring the gap between what they saw and reality, or maybe reality did not exist and everything was interpretation. These entangled misconceptions allowed for mutual understanding.

Often, Gus feared Prosp was bored. Of all the experiences he had shown Prosp by removing him from his environment, this was the one for which he most chastised himself. He did not believe auks in the wild to be capable of boredom, any more than a giraffe or a sparrow. Boredom was the purview of humans and their pets—dogs, cats, and horses—corresponding to the repetition of days where they had no need to fend for their survival. But Prosp could spend hours in his basin or watching the light move and flicker about. A fish circling the water was enough to engage his curiosity; well-fed, he played like a cat with its prey. Perhaps Gus was mistaken. In the end, everything around Prosp must, in fact, intrigue and surprise him. After all, he did things no other great auk before him had done, like pose for a portrait, observe Augustine and Ottarr as they came over to play, listen to evening discussions between humans around a flowerpot in the greenhouse.

WHILE HIS COLLEAGUE HANSEN BELIEVED THAT the two very last wild specimens of the great auk had been killed on Eldey, rumours had sprung up and were making the rounds, carried from boat to boat, from conversation to conversation in the ports: Great auks had been spotted who knows where now, probably near St. Kilda—then: Yes, it was St. Kilda, without a doubt. If one were to believe the fishers and travellers, the sea was teeming with great auks. But these snatches of stories from some professor or member of the Royal Academy of Sciences were always somewhat vague, passed down from the friend of a friend who had spotted a largish black and white shape in the distance waddling along the beach of a storm-battered rock, or on a wave as it broke under the swell of another.

Hansen merely shrugged when Gus reported back on these stories, until one day when Gus told him about a naturalist for the University of Durham, in England, one William Proctor. Proctor had searched for great auks all over Iceland and, as of 1837, having failed to find one, had pronounced the great auk extinct. However, of course, Proctor was wrong, since on Eldey in 1844 the pair of auks had been killed. Hansen was forced to refine his opinion. After all, he couldn't be sure of anything either.

"I cannot prove absence," he said to Gus, "I would have to be God, and view the entire world in the blink of an eye. Their non-presence is unverifiable. You will have to demonstrate the presence of these auks somewhere."

And so Gus promised to set out again soon in search of

Prosp's comrades. Yet he kept stalling. He feared disappointment, a fruitless expedition, hours lost surveying distant shadows, confusing a dolphin's fin or a whale's back with an auk's silhouette. He dreaded returning while, looking at Prosp, he imagined a hypothetical great auk stuffed and transported from one museum to the next, "Here it is, the very last specimen."

In 1847, while the portrait painter worked on a likeness of Ottarr, a year after finishing Augustine's, in which Ottarr, to imitate his sister, had demanded to pose with a dog—borrowed from a neighbour—there was a great auk sighting in Iceland, then again in Norway. Gus felt that Iceland, as expansive and deserted as it was, offered the perfect refuge; it no longer seemed absurd to remain hopeful.

One evening, one of his students brought him a copy of Audubon's *Birds of America*, in an abridged edition: a book of splendid drawings of all the birds from the continent in purportedly natural poses, observed in the wild, though Audubon had also painted the cadavers of animals he had killed in considerable numbers in order to miss no detail of their plumage. Isolated as he had been on the Faroes, Gus had missed the book's tremendous success.

The student had bookmarked the page with a great auk. Its portrait, like all of Audubon's, was drawn with a thin line, a drawing that no word could describe more aptly than "delicate." The harmonious colours, here in tones of grey and pale purple, seemed a touch sad next to the vibrant yellows, the reds, and the blues used for the other species (except for birds of prey). Two great auks appeared in profile, one upright on land, the other in the water against a background Gus found absurd and an attempt at Japanese-style painting, a tiny landscape of tiny waves and bordered by beige bluffs.

"It's all wrong!" said Gus, who would have liked to give

a measured response, but was for the moment too jealous. "He made it look like a farm bird. It looks like an idiot—see how round it is?" And it was true. Prosp, in real life, looked more dangerous, more hostile.

"He didn't encounter any great auks. It's drawn from description," said the student. "He couldn't see one in the wild, since they had already disappeared from North America."

To Gus, the whole drawing brought to mind a tomb, a dumbstruck, obliging bird in a pond, half duck, half turkey, impossible to imagine as a good swimmer. Of course Gus had drawn Prosp a hundred times, in much more authentic and much more surprising postures that highlighted the auk's capricious moods and emotional depths. True, Audubon's lines had a charm that his lacked, and his colours, though bleak, were pleasing, and his engravings as a whole evoked the peace of a harmonious world, but their elegant pallor rendered a grotesque unrealism. What peace was this, exactly? What peace could this creature enjoy, at the brink of its extinction?

The next morning *Birds of America* lay open to the offending page on a buffet in the dining room, under the portrait of Augustine and Prosp. Gus was sitting at the head of the table. The whole family had been called in to compare the two—to Audubon's disfavour—and to take offence at this immense affront to great auks. Gus, in his shirt sleeves, dishevelled, face drawn and white as though his fixation were draining him of blood, let everyone have their say. Ottarr admitted to finding the engraving "pretty," while sticking his fingers into his cup. Augustine did not see the resemblance with Prosp. And, finally, once she had a slice of toast with jam in hand, Elinborg noted, "It's quite bland. It makes me think of a pet bird in someone's sitting room, or a Christmas roast laid out on a table."

Gus relaxed. The Prosp in the family portrait, now *he* commanded respect. Next to the seated child smiling somewhat slyly at the artist, Prosp appeared enormous. His beak streaked with light-coloured stripes looked as though it could rip open the child's cheek, juxtaposed with Augustine's peaceful gaze, her tangled hair, casual in her everyday dress, an oversized cup in her hand, as though both of them had been snatched up mid-snack. She was looking away from Prosp, which was normal, since she was not afraid of him. He had been there before the painter arrived in the room and would be there after.

The sightings of great auks continued. There was even a sighting in Newfoundland, a place the species had officially deserted at the start of the century. The rumour came from the docks, from the taverns. The price of any relic, the tiniest piece of animal, soared. Gus lurked in pubs and inns, where he hoped for once to find some first-hand information. But it never came. The man who'd seen the bird was never the one to tell how a brother, a cousin, or niece of Prosp's had come into view.

Until one day a sailor told Gus of a sale he'd made to someone from the Museum of Copenhagen, the entrails of two auks off Eldey that he and some others had killed four years earlier in 1844. He had no idea who'd taken the skins, a thought that still sent him into a rage. It was surely those dishonest other three sailors, or, more likely, the ship's captain, who'd played them for fools. The man had a scar like a shiny red hill in the middle of his lower lip from a careless harpoon swing. He couldn't say why anyone would want the entrails; nothing more he could tell Gus. Gus thought of his university colleagues and felt sick to his stomach. Some of them had likely tried to pet Prosp when they came to the house, right after observing the intestines of a great auk floating in formaldehyde.

"Do you think there are still great auks out there somewhere?" he asked the mariner.

"Surely not. I, Ketill Ketilsson, saw the last two. Remember that name."

Gus would indeed remember; he even intended to leave it in his notes for posterity, so he wrote the name in capital letters and underlined it. Though what did some man named Ketilsson's opinion matter in face of the belief that all creation, even in the absence of God, moved toward betterment, progress, justice? It did not, of course. Gus continued to believe that there were Prosps out there alive somewhere, though he was no fool. He knew how to count: one bird here, another there. Two breeding auks did not make a population, only the last of the species, whose reproduction could never stem their depletion, and would, in fact, irrevocably engender their extinction.

The rumours scarcened. Months passed, then years. No one saw any more great auks, near or far. The subject, even the name, had fallen from conversation in the ports and university hallways. It was as if great auks had never existed, as though the relics were no longer of interest, or else that the birds were living quietly in great numbers in the middle of the oceans, and so what was the use in speaking of them?

Prosp was growing older. His black feathers no longer turned white, his beak no longer frittered away but stiffened, and he appeared weary—or, at least, so it appeared to Gus. In winter, when his basin froze over, he had few things to do, shut away in the greenhouse, unsteady on land, and required more pitchers of water on his dried-out plumage. He was still a great auk, but again, in Gus's view, an altered one—

an isolated one. Every morning, he ran to Gus or Elinborg, sometimes to Augustine then Ottarr, with wings behind his back, beak forward, and belly more or less facing the ground, to angle for the fish they freely fed him.

After supper, he stayed sitting in the circle with Gus and Elinborg and the students, who were used to him by now and no longer viewed him as a wild animal. Of course, one wondered what Prosp understood, as he stood perfectly straight and gazed through half-closed eyes, sometimes ejecting a sort of convincing gobbling sound or an authoritarian caw amid the conversation, no doubt his version of a meaningful opinion, which everyone respected. It was akin to a cat's meow or a parrot's squawk—a parrot from some tropical place. Prosp stood out against the almost-urban landscape, in the shrubs in the garden, on the grass near his basin. When they looked over at him, the anomaly felt amusing, almost as if he were an attraction: a monkey at the market, or one of Audubon's inaccurate drawings come to life.

Then one night, Prosp slipped on a stone slab more uneven than the others on the greenhouse floor and tripped as he hit the next tile with his claws. A student named Rasmussen burst out laughing. Prosp was wiggling on the floor, struggling to get back up, which happened rarely. Gus grabbed Prosp and set him on his feet, as Rasmussen kept roaring with laughter. He poked fun at Prosp as though he were a tiger who'd just missed a hoop at the circus, miming the bird falling and slipping across the wet floor, then fleeing, vexed, under a table across the room, out of sight. Gus's hands shook. He thought he could see the auk redden, ashamed or embarrassed.

Rasmussen, who never apologized, was not invited back. Why would he apologize for laughing at an animal? At the zoo, people supposedly had a good laugh at the otariids, ignorant of what graceful swimmers they were, how they hunted in the ocean. So why would the caprice of some professor be less amusing, his whim for an animal maladapted to domestication, this farce of a wild beast—a seabird whose feathers were used to stuff duvets—who, even in water, would never scare a soul, less than a seal or a dolphin or shark, at least?

Now each time Gus observed Prosp in the garden near his basin, he saw Prosp's existence shrivelling due to his own actions, an artificial, anemic life where everything must have the pale taste of the already-dead fish Prosp ate, the still waters he bathed in. He kept imagining Prosp slipping on the polished floors in the house, getting back up without understanding why he was so poorly made for this place, with no wings to fly like the pigeons that rested in the trees, the palms he had for feet, encumbering, oversized, which knocked together when he would have liked to leap as a cat did or have legs to run like a child.

When ideas of this kind seized him, Gus felt his tongue swell, in want of saliva. He would think again how great auks must still exist someplace, since Prosp existed, because Prosp had survived. There was never just a single miracle in the universe. Isolated miracles only happened in stories, or the Bible. In nature, of such great vastness, where shapes repeated, cycles started over, nothing was new, everything reappearing, sometimes with tiny variations, but reappearing nonetheless.

This is why he decided to return to the taverns, skulk around the docks, spy on cargo being unloaded from the ships. He drank at market stalls, devoured bowls of stew on oil-slicked tables. He questioned the mariners all night, until one day one of them said, yes, he had happened on a colony of great auks, ten or so, in Iceland, northwest in the Vestfirðir region. In fact, he happened to have a relic in his pocket, and he was hoping to sell it to a collector in Copenhagen.

The man's small, hard, sunken blue eyes were the only thing that moved on a face pulled tight by lines running in every direction, as though contrary movements had cancelled out all motion. Gus wanted to see the relic. The man slid from his pocket the tip of a long beak, stripes etched into it like ravines, identical to Prosp's, the same size and equally hard when he knocked it against the table edge. He hadn't killed the bird, he explained, just bought the beak in Reykjavik from a merchant with no sense of its worth. The man asked nothing of Gus, refusing even to let him pay for both drinks.

As he left, Gus knew he would not sleep at all that night, and not much the nights after either. He knew that from that evening onward he would dream of arid lands, endless grass, just as he had dreamed of trees before he'd left the Faroes. He knew he would toss and turn in his bedsheets as he looked out into the darkness of his bedroom to see Prosp's silhouette multiplying on a rocky beach. As of that night, as soon as he closed his eyes, eerie blue glaciers would glow all around him, and he would make out Prosp's black and white shape near the base, walking toward other great auks, and then, only the daffodil yellow of his beak open with the joy of summer.

This was why—to sleep again, to make Prosp happy, but for the adventure of it too—Gus decided to leave. Organizing the voyage was simple enough; the Academy and the University regularly sent out exploration teams to Iceland. Elinborg agreed with his going. The prospect of the lonely days—the months—she would spend without him was exasperating, but she had thought it through and saw no way to refuse it. In one sense, it was a kind of moral contract between them and marital protocol: Gus and science, Gus and Prosp, in spite of the children.

And Elinborg told herself it was because Gus loved Prosp that he also loved Ottarr and Augustine, as he had devoted his entire person to a fragile creature—for whom one day he'd taken on, almost by chance, responsibility—and thus he could be trusted with the children, whom he took care of less and less as they grew older. She had understood in the end that Prosp showed Gus's ability to love wholly, a kindness born of a difference so complete, to such an extent that it cannot be entirely understood, a respect for something that cannot be but protected and cherished since its fate has been placed in your hands. Elinborg also remembered how she had met an adventurer on a barren archipelago barely anyone visited, a man who'd lived there with her in cramped quarters in a simplicity bordering on poverty, and that they had been happy together. Keeping him here, among the paved streets of a clean city, the false collars and smell of laundry, the gentle lagoons, made little sense to her.

Two months later, Gus boarded a vessel with Prosp that would drop him in Iceland before continuing to Canada. Elinborg and the children stood on the dock waving their handkerchiefs, and Gus blew kisses from the boat. In his arms, the auk let out joyful cries, goodbyes that felt like a promise of reunion. Soon Gus could see only small dots in the distance but could still make out his wife's light grey skirt as the wind rustled it and Ottarr's cap flying off his head and after it, fast as he was able, his son must have been racing to catch it.

ON A BOAT PURCHASED IN THE PORT WHERE HE DISembarked, he sailed along the south coast, then the coast to the west. No great auks along the way. By day, Prosp sat near the prow, chest puffed like a proud mariner, or posed standing, his belly covering his feet and his eyes closed. At night he slept next to Gus. The cabin was so small Gus could extend his arm and rest a hand on the bird's back in the dark, as though to be sure he was not alone, that he had a friend. Prosp would let out a short coo of surprise, then fall back asleep. Gus knew they were of mutual comfort to each other in this shared closeness, this affinity neither would have with another of their own species.

They stopped off in fishing villages. Gus inquired about great auks, but no one had seen any in years. He spoke to older residents who remembered sightings in their youth. Some of them had even eaten auk meat, but it was such a long time ago, they'd forgotten how it tasted. The boat landed in Reykjavik. Finding the man he had heard about in Denmark took only three days of questioning the mariners disembarking in the port, telling them he was a collector in search of auk skins. The man was a well-known outfitter who owned a shop and a boat. In truth, Gus could have skipped the pretence. Selling auk relics was not illegal, and no one cared why a Frenchman should want a foot or feathers or a skin, so long as he had the coin for it.

The shop's walls were covered in tools, fish hooks, and nets, the floor littered with baskets, coats, and hats. Helgason had been expecting the Frenchman. He smiled, old and affable.

He was nearly half Gus's height and took out a beak and three rib bones almost at once, from a desk in the back. Gus pretended to examine them and, to draw out the exchange, inquired as to whether he had, by chance, a skin. Helgason said, yes, he might do, he'd have to have a look, but if Gus liked notable, even spectacular objects, he might even have an egg around still. They'd be more expensive, of course—the skin and the egg both.

The man went into the back. Gus heard the rustle of boxes, drawers opening and shutting. When he returned, he had a bag full of fresh feathers, beautiful ones, still soft. Gus felt as though he were touching a smooth, supple Prosp, like the real Prosp, who'd have covered his entire hand in caresses—a cloud or a whisper of Prosp, skinless and boneless. If Gus came back the next day, Helgason said, he'd surely have found the egg. With all this junk lying about the place, he didn't know where he'd put it.

Asking Helgason where he hunted auks, he realized, would be as futile as asking a gold miner the location of his lode. Did he have any other recent items? Gus was only interested in newer relics like the feathers. Helgason's mouth, quite earnestly, puckered into a near perfect circle on finding the Frenchman so stupid, showing he risked vexing him with his epic ignorance.

"The feathers have been washed. It's understandable you thought them new. They're quite old, in fact—proof to their fine quality."

The small man smiled, and his mouth once again took on the shape of a friendly human expression. Gus looked over the ribs again, layered thick and almost stuck together with dust, and the beak with a blunted point and stripes dulled like the eroded crests of a mountain.

"Don't you go to the Vestfirðir every year to find birds?"

"Why would I do that? Look at me. Too far, at my age."

Gus buckled under his words, as though a beam had come down on his shoulders. How could he have thought it would be so simple? That he'd be able to walk into a shop and ask for a skin, and he'd find a fresh one just three days old?

"When did you get these?"

Gus, in truth, wanted to ask "where" but the words were muddled in his mind. "Where" became "when," and "how" was "what," and "what" had no utility. He knew "what" was only this beak, these rib bones, these feathers.

"Over fifteen years ago now. You'd still see them around these parts, then. I was young. We'd catch them. These are a few old pieces I keep as mementos. Now I sell them. I could find that egg. I don't think I sold it, but I can't be too sure. At one time, everyone was looking for them, I seem to remember. But I might be confusing things."

Helgason looked as crestfallen as Gus for a moment, but no doubt for him it was the sadness of life, where one always grows older, and the things one once did with joy, which made for an existence to be proud of, have gone. As for Gus, he saw his hopes drop to the cluttered shop floor and slither away between two jute bags.

Never would Prosp enjoy a companion other than Gus, nor would Gus be the man who'd saved the great auk. He'd had his chance on Eldey on meeting Prosp, but had watched that chance go by and missed it. He should have let the bird escape in the water that day and, who knows, breed somewhere else, or he should have stopped the sailors from attacking; yes, he should have paid them to steer the ship away without stopping ashore.

Even though he had been sickened by the slaughter, he had done nothing. He had watched the despicable, gratuitous scene—gratuitous, since no one was hungry. As he had watched the corpses pile up, the total of corpses being equal to the total of the few birds living on the island had not perturbed him. At the time, he had only thought of how he would send the captured bird to Paris, and there, too, he had not revolted, until his chance had passed him by. He remembered the birds crying out, the bloodstains on the rocks at Eldey, which, from afar, shone and stickied the bodies hanging from the mariners' hands. He had been useless to Prosp.

Gus had to sit down on a nearby stool. If someone had walked into the shop at that moment, they'd have seen two men in the same slumped position, on either side of the counter, two pairs of eyes staring into space, hovering over an invisible drawing on the ground that must have recounted the story of two early adulthoods that had never crossed paths, with the only thing in common being their end. One had stopped fishing whales and penguins and auks, and the other had never fished whales or penguins and only once auks, which he regretted. One asked himself, in a daze, how he had ended up selling tools instead of steering a ship, how he had ended up hunched and shrunken when once he had been tall, agile, strong; and the other was stunned to find his life had been spent paddling around the North Sea basin, when he had planned, as a young man, to explore the Pacific and the sprawling expanses of Australia rather than deserted islands toward the Arctic.

Gus ambled through the streets of Reykjavik, nodding as though in response to himself or some demon. He had an anomaly in his charge, a creature unlike any other in existence. He struggled, amazed, waved a hand in front of him as though refuting some argument, dropping his head again, perplexed. He had an animal that didn't exist, or rather, one like a griffin, a fantastical beast like from a dream, an animal fit to be engraved on a medallion.

How was this possible? The whales and seals lived on. In Africa, there were enormous, and no doubt stupid, rhinoceroses, swaggering beasts that would probably have made a nice stew. And in Australia an incredible animal, a farce of nature: a beaver with a duck's bill, which, more surprising still, laid eggs though it was a mammal and nursed its young, yet this absurd beast, not even pretty, lived on while Prosp's kind, so harmless and funny and such graceful swimmers, had disappeared. Where was the justice? Beyond that: Where was the harmony? As he left the city to get back to the boat, he began to wave his arms above his head, and people paused to look at him and laugh.

Aboard the boat, he calmed down. He and Prosp would leave the next day. There was no reason to stay on. They would go to the Vestfirðir, a region near empty of human settlements where the last living great auks might have been sighted long ago. It would be a pilgrimage, a return to the lands of origin before extinction. They would take in the oceans and the beaches, where every wave, every grain of sand would be like the leaning gravestone in a cemetery no longer visited.

At first he dared not look at Prosp as he prepared the boat. He was ashamed. He did not know how to communicate this strange and unreasonable thing happening to Prosp: He was the last of his kind on earth, and he was—it might as well be stated as such—the last living great auk in the world, in spite of the vastness and wonder of this world, the millions of others it could have sheltered. A creature with a unique destiny: the last to know the sensations, the language, the instincts of his species—the last in all of the non-eternity of great auks to remember over five thousand years they had spent on the earth.

THEY ARRIVED IN NORTHWESTERN ICELAND IN THE summer of 1849. They moved into a one-room house near the water, built of stone and turf. The house would hold in the heat in winter. The closest village was fourteen kilometres away. It was just the two of them, on the rocks and the plains, but then they were used to that. They were alone, and both the last, in a sense: Gus, the last man on earth to see a great auk, and Prosp, the last of his kind.

The days lasted twenty hours in summer, four in winter. Sometimes at night Gus woke and saw Prosp's outline, resting like a duck at the foot of his bed. He'd reach a tired hand out toward him, rest it on his body, and the sleeping auk would let out his short coo of surprise then quiet again, reassured since the hand was Gus's, since when they were next to one another everything was all right. And Gus would fall back asleep, too, feeling safe because he had the bird to protect him.

They fished together, Gus in the boat, of course, and Prosp in the water. Prosp swallowed what he caught, and Gus brought his catch ashore. The auk would watch him cook in the evenings—before, Prosp had never come into the kitchen. At first, he'd steal bits from Gus's plate, and Gus would pretend not to notice. After a few weeks, Gus would hold his fork out to Prosp while he ate supper, and Prosp would take the food on the end of it. It became a ritual. Both were happy for Prosp to stop stealing things.

Gus believed his presence comforted his lonely bird. Which was ridiculous since Prosp did not know he was the last living auk, nor that he was swimming in a mausoleum. He had almost only ever known Gus and his family; life among other auks was foreign to him. Quite frankly, it did not for a single second occur to Prosp that he could have lived any other way.

For the first period of their new life, Gus would sometimes wonder which one of the two of them was human and which one a bird. It was as though, because they had spent all this time together and had shared habits, they had created a hybrid species, a chimera of seabird and man. When he looked in the mirror, Gus no longer really recognized himself. His beard and hair had grown out and, other than his forehead, ears, hands, and cheekbones, when he was dressed, not one bit of skin showed. Prosp did not recognize himself in a mirror either and, since there were no other auks, must have been indifferent to his appearance.

Sometimes on the beach they would spot an orca's fin or a rorqual's tail in the distance. And Prosp would race away from the water as though mad, crying out, rushing back to snap at Gus's pant leg so they could retreat to the shelter of the shore. Gus found this amusing—how could he not? And touching, too, for he saw that Prosp did not desert him, despite their intermingling of existences, the auk with his particular and unwavering instinct, and himself, a human, unafraid of what lived in water and could not reach solid ground.

Why was Gus still there at the ends of the earth? He could not say. Something had left his nerves in shreds, and he could now only manage the basics of his routine: fishing, sleeping, eating, petting Prosp, walking with Prosp, watching him dive and swim in the water. When Gus thought about it, all else felt pointless. When he thought of Elinborg and the children, he saw faces in a painting on the wall of a well-lit house, a setting that went right through the ghost of a man he no longer was.

Nobody needed him. His fate was an odd one, more incredible for his banal existence in the face of such an exceptional event: the end of a species. He had searched and failed to find a similar tale, a similar experience of any person. The death of the last dodo was known long after its extinction. No doubt the entire species had died without anyone being aware of it, with no one to worry. There was an idea, for instance, about when the last mammoth had died, but Gus was willing to wager that no single hunter had wondered where they'd gone. Populations declined slowly, and the memory of them was erased. How could such a thing be comprehended? How could one truly grasp that something that had existed, had been numerous, had proliferated, was suddenly wiped out?

Prosp was there, in front of him, swimming. Just the day before he had fought for his life, after a narrow escape with an Arctic fox that had pounced on him. Its white fur had blended in with the snow, Prosp hadn't seen it coming. The fox had squashed him like a pancake, and Prosp had fought it off by biting so hard that the stunned fox found itself with a bloodied neck as it ran to escape the livid seabird in pursuit with his impressive beak open wide. And yet notwithstanding this courage, this recklessness, Prosp would soon disappear. He would not just die, which was the natural order of things; no, he would dissolve and along with him every trace of his kind's existence, of a way of being, of eating, of defending, of loving, perhaps. And it was shocking that Gus was the only one to know. Not even Prosp was aware.

Gus felt like he was in some sort of dream. "Why me, someone who held no interest in the subject, why am I even aware of this? Why am I the one here?" And every time he had this thought—every day—he felt himself levitate above the hills and look down to see hordes of animals with blurred outlines move from one place to another in the night, right up to the void of the sky, one long line of uncertain shapes that was suddenly tugged from the earth and traversing the dark space toward the moon.

Winter came. Gus was having trouble walking. His breathing had become laboured, his legs leaden. Often he wondered if his seabird should not leave and live its life for once, the life of a great auk. Except the life of a great auk was a concept of yore, an inert idea, which, like him, had run out of stamina by the first syllable.

Everything Gus cast his eyes upon that winter seemed to grow threadbare. He remembered a blanket Elinborg had made on the Faroes and had stored in a trunk for the summer. Months later, when she took it out, she found it ravaged by moths, entire stripes of colour missing; here, the great auks were missing, too, from this moth-eaten landscape. Who would remember Prosp? Who would remember those like Prosp and their grace underwater, their fumbling on land, the strength of their jaws as they cracked open crustaceans, their amity, their quickness to anger?

Gus spent more and more time in bed. He still travelled to the village every two weeks for provisions, and fished every three days, but everything had become arduous in the cold and drizzle. Prosp seemed in poor humour. By day he would stay on the beach, ambivalent as to where Gus was. Then he would swim, first for two hours, then three, then six. But he was far from living the normal life of an auk, since auks spent months at sea. No doubt Prosp, too, was tired and, for some time now, not entirely auk, which was what Gus had begun to fear back in Denmark.

When Prosp returned to shore, Gus was often sleeping, and, suddenly reconciled, the seabird would jump on the bed and plunk down next to the pillow. In the morning, Gus would wake up with his mouth pasty, his legs somewhat stiff.

One day Prosp, vexed by his lethargy, bit the back of his leg. Gus wondered whether the gesture were friendly, to bring him to reality, or a mean-spirited manifestation of Prosp's annoyance. He did not consider it further. Another morning, Gus coughed up blood and went back to bed. Prosp tried to get him out again, this time pecking at his arm. His beak was hard and cold, its force painful and pointed. Gus merely turned over to face the wall, and when he lifted his head a few moments later, he saw Prosp, feathers ruffled on his back, waddle toward the door and leave without looking back.

Prosp did not come back, neither the next day nor the following ones. Gus pulled himself from his bed and spent a few hours a day on the shore waiting for his auk. Once he thought he saw Prosp. A surge of relief, his muscles relaxing, made him want to jump up and down on the beach to show Prosp he was there, waiting. But it was not after all a great auk in the water, but a seal. There was bitter disappointment. Coming back to the house, he coughed up blood again.

Gus was burning up. The sheet, his nightshirt, and the plaid coverlet felt impossibly heavy, but when he took them off the cold was unbearable, so he pulled them back on, laid his coat over them; he felt the covers were as a statue, heavy as marble. He slept all day and night. Soon he lost all sense of distinction between outside and inside; it was cold everywhere and always dark. The fever left him drenched, his long hair stuck to his forehead, a sour smell of damp and sweat. No other human ventured into this remote, glacial place, not even for winter activities. When he woke, for fifteen minutes or so, he thought he must be the only man on earth—the last of his kind too. His arms were still bruised from Prosp's furious beak, before the auk had left. Gus thought he saw the marks moving, expanding, pulsating like parasites under his skin.

In his lucid moments, he thought of Elinborg and the

children, and tried to calculate how long it would take for them to learn of his death. No doubt it would be before summer, when someone might chance upon the house. He thought he could hear a storm outside, but perhaps it was only the usual wind. Soon he had lost the strength to open his eyes. In any case, there was nothing to see in that hideous room. He barely dreamed. Everything he saw asleep was reality, only contorted, rubbery: the walls around him softening into mush, a rorqual knocking against an auk under the water, his bed sinking into the floor, a deserted man on top of it, drowning, it seemed, in a sea of oil, and alone, without his auk, who was alone as well.

One day, he had a strange sensation. Something viscous and cold seemed to be resting on his forehead. It was supple and smooth, but not unpleasant. Like everything else, it smelled of the sea. Formulating that thought felt reassuring in itself, since it proved he was not in such a bad way, as he was able to analyze an element outside of himself. But why would this thing, viscous, cold and smooth, want to lie on his forehead? No. He must be delirious still. The thing was still there. It slid from his forehead down to his ear. Come to think of it, it was somewhat rough as well, like a fish, he would have said. But how could a fish have left the water and reached his pillow? If he could only open his eyes once and for all. But he did not have the strength. He fell back to sleep.

When Gus awoke, a warm, gentle pulse as warm as Prosp's feathers clung to his cheek. For a moment, remembering Prosp, he thought he would have liked to explain what was happening, to him, the great auk. He would have apologized for having put him in this situation of being still alive when all of his kind had disappeared; he would have apologized for not having found him a companion when it was still possible, for having thus transformed Prosp into the cranky old bird he had become. The bird who had, to punish Gus, left.

Gus could taste saltwater on his lips, but of course everything tasted of salt there. It must be his own tears. Yet he felt better. Then he heard a tiny cry, of surprise or hope. And the soft elongated curve of a plumed neck touching his ear and his temples. At the end of the neck, there was something solid, something that resembled the hardness of a beak—Prosp's. He had to open his eyes, he had to check whether Prosp had returned, but he feared he would find himself alone. He felt so calm with what he thought to be Prosp at his side, the loving Prosp who had come back, with such small, fine, soft feathers covering him. He heard a sharp cry again, which no doubt recounted in auk, "Open your eyes. It's me. Go on. You've nothing to fear."

And Gus opened his eyes. Prosp's head was leaned against his own, beak touching his nose, eyes staring straight into Gus's own. Gus lifted his hands to put his arms around the bird's warm body. He cried, but tears of joy, and Prosp cried out softly, as though murmuring a song. To the left of the pillow was a fish, which the auk grabbed and placed near Gus's mouth. Gus had not eaten in a long time. Then, exhausted, he slept again, a hand on the back of the animal who'd saved him and continued to croon.

Gus got better. He began to walk again. His legs were still heavy, but his joints moved more easily. He sometimes spoke to himself, often as he nodded. Prosp seemed to be watching him; was he aware? Surely the auk had a broad understanding of humans but lacked the details. It was Prosp who fed Gus for a good month. He would fish and bring back his catch, and Gus would cook or dry them. Prosp had become his doctor, and the head of the house.

In the spring, and feeling better, Gus travelled to the village for provisions. His relations with the villagers were wholly laconic. He had lost all desire for conversation. When he got home, Prosp was waiting. Gus needed Prosp, and he felt that Prosp, too, needed him. They were two madmen who'd extricated themselves from society, two magical creatures from the time of Merlin, hermits at the ends of a forest no human crossed, two mementos of days of yore now gone where anything living held the same weight, where Prosp, since he was alive, resembled Gus, who resembled a bee, which resembled a blade of grass and the numbing snow in winter.

One day they came across a little auk—a razorbill—while walking. Essentially a smaller version of Prosp with real wings. Prosp froze in shock on the beach, several metres from the rock where the razorbill had paused. He reacted as when he had first seen a cat in Denmark: He submitted before this creature with an unknown smell and shape—assuming he could perceive its shape—sound, and capabilities of defence or attack. Yet the razorbill was not so different than him, at least from Gus's perspective; yet who knows how Prosp saw himself.

Neither bird was hostile, though. The razorbill seemed indifferent, in fact. After stopping short, Prosp approached, his neck jutting toward the other bird. This time, the razorbill appeared startled. Prosp stopped a couple metres away in order to, without frightening the creature, contemplate the marvellous reproduction of himself, clumsy as him on land and as agile with its beak, which at that moment was scratching the feathers on its belly.

Prosp let out a cry Gus had never heard him make: a deep, heavy sound that hung in the air, a sound almost of despair, with his throat and head craned skyward, body tensed and narrowed by the effort, still vibrating after its final note. The razorbill stopped grooming itself. Gus dared not move. He heard the sob again, like the wail of a prisoner freed after twenty years and perceiving the world had changed completely. The razorbill agitated its wings, not much larger than those of a pigeon, but enormous compared to Prosp's appendages. Prosp imitated the movement as though he wanted to persuade the razorbill he too could fly, that until now, stupid as he was, he had stupidly taken these accessories for fins; or else he was just being polite, trying to be friendly and show his goodwill. The bird puffed its chest and flew off. Prosp watched him go several seconds then stared back again at the deserted rock, emitted another cry, a complaint that echoed the first, deep and long. Gus felt sure Prosp was crying.

They went home. Gus had to carry Prosp, as he refused to leave the rock the razorbill had flown from. At supper, the auk did not wait for food from Gus's fork. He stood completely still in a corner of their one room. He did not sleep, nor cry, nor even murmur. Gus rested his hands on Prosp's feathers, but to no effect. The great auk remained sitting upright, eyes fixed on the wall that was now almost obscured by the night—such a fixed gaze that it seemed almost as though he had gone blind.

No animal can be alone on this earth. And no person, either, thought Gus, lest they become like Prosp, swaying their head back and forth and uttering sentences randomly, and eventually losing language altogether, emitting a whistle to speak to a tree's leaves, to the dust, to the mice nibbling in corners of a single room. Prosp, who had not known his comrades and who perceived that no creature resembled him, was the loneliest creature that had ever existed. He had no hands, so he was not human; he had no functioning wings, so he was not a razorbill.

Every time he approached any life form, he must have

felt his terrible peculiarity. He was a marine animal, and in the end spent little time in the ocean. He was a great auk on the decline, cut off from the life force of his species. If he died then and there, his species would meet a sad end: a death between four walls of a house, jealous of a miserable razorbill nowhere near as majestic.

The next day they went back to the water. They looked out to the horizon, at the birds nesting on the cliffs. Even the foxes, Prosp's sworn enemies, were once again brown. Prosp had no reaction on seeing them. Mammals, beasts confined to land, no longer held any interest for him. He was no longer afraid of them. They stayed awhile to look out at the water as far as they could see—an hour, then three. They were quiet, but it seemed to Gus like they were talking, recounting stories of underwater cities, of battles with rorquals, of racing alongside the seals. They would see white bears, too, near the shoreline; they were very dangerous, agile swimmers in the water, and Prosp and Gus tried not to look at them, in hopes of going unnoticed. Once, Prosp had swum out and come up against a gannet darting into the water. Its beak had hit Prosp's head and the two swam away stunned, Prosp thrown off course, both losing the coveted fish.

They compared the thickness of the seaweed, the taste of cod and crustaceans. Perhaps Prosp remembered the warmth of his parents' bellies when his egg hatched, the taste of food regurgitated into his throat, the cold of his first swim, the strength it had taken to survive it, his first—and only—trip across the sea with his kin, when they had spent the winter in the ocean before coming back to Eldey months later.

They had swum out in a row into the abyss, floated out far into the sea with no land in sight. They had passed albatrosses, without knowing what they were, and gulls, near every day. They had not liked the gulls, for no reason they could name, but likely due to their irritating cries. Once Prosp had escaped the jaws of a whale. He had felt a pressure and the rush of water across his belly; he had turned sharp across the creature's nose. Later, he watched one of his kind devoured in his place. That was a great auk's existence.

Prosp rested his neck against Gus's leg. It was the first display of affection since they had seen the razorbill. Gus caressed him. Prosp's neck wrapped around Gus's hand; Gus's hand wrapped around Prosp's body, and Prosp cooed. The deep sound vibrated in his chest, and Gus sang a lullaby he had learned on the Faroes, a sad, guttural song, slow and deep. He had not realized he still remembered it. It was the song that most resembled the song of the auks, to what he imagined was their language.

Prosp disentangled himself. Gus placed his hand back on his own knee. The auk slowly waded out, like a man stepping into the ocean to bathe. The water up to his chest, he turned to Gus. And Gus sat there frozen, apart from his hand, which he waved, because that is how his kind says goodbye and gives themselves strength. The gesture showed Prosp that he understood—he understood it was best. Prosp turned to look ahead and inched forward. Gus watched Prosp's back. Prosp dove in. This time, he did not come back.

FOR TWO YEARS GUS WAITED FOR PROSP TO RETURN. Every day, he sat on a menhir-shaped rock tilted on its side to make a bench. Though after half an hour he was numbed by the cold, he would keep squinting at the beach. One June day, he saw a boat lay anchor in the bay. A man paddled over in a rowboat and stepped ashore.

He recognized Buchanan at once. He had been waiting for Elinborg to send the Scotsman to find him. Buchanan had not changed, his face still oblong as cuttlebone washed up in the waves. Gus let him sit down next to him, but he did not want to talk, only to pretend he had not noticed him arrive.

"Gus, I'm here to bring you home."

Straight to the point.

A salt-worn, salt-stained image appeared before Gus: The woman he had married and his children pressed their hands up against the cloudy glass, as though they were going to lift it up and carry it away. He could barely make out their features. There was a drollness, a pathos to the scene. How naive they were, how confident that their thin grey shadows could affect him, how certain of their intentions. He would never leave this place, not the beach he sat on all day nor the house he retired to when he had to rest. Everything he looked at trembled. He knew he had begun to lean his head to one side and the other, then back again. Why would he go home like this, dishevelled, his vision shaky, reeking of fish and never wanting to be rid of the smell? He did not want to leave Prosp. He did not want to give up on the possibility of seeing Prosp surface from a wave and wash up on the beach to greet him.

"Gus, you know I loved Prosp too. But it's time to come home. At least till you're well. Look at you. You're shaking. And I reckon your teeth are falling out."

But no, Gus had not lost a single tooth. He grimaced, and stared out to sea, more determined. He wanted to pretend Buchanan wasn't there.

Often he saw Prosp in his dreams, stretched out on the beach. The auk would lift his head then rest it wearily back down at the edge of a lapping wave. Gus could see the shallow breath in the bird's chest, his pulse slowing. A few gulls were perched farther out, and quite near, a group of crows waited to scavenge. Gus would wake up gasping.

He felt Buchanan's shoulder knock against his. He needed to focus. Was Buchanan on the beach with Prosp too? If so he must have been near the crows. But where was Gus? No doubt lying next to Prosp in the seafoam. Gus needed to gather the strength to explain why he wouldn't leave, why it had been a waste of time for Buchanan to come, how futile it was to play a scavenger hoping to drag his corpse from the bench. How could he tell Buchanan that he hated him for coming here? Though he had to admit the Scotsman was kind—were Scotsmen a species in their own right? Gus pondered this for the first time. Before, way back when, Gus had been a person like any other. He knew the answer without having to formulate words: Scotsmen belonged to the human species, same as the Danish, or the Japanese on the other side of the globe. Could a globe truly have a side? These kinds of thoughts were exhausting. Here is what he must say to Buchanan: that his presence had caused Gus to reflect on useless and tiresome subjects. If he wanted to help, since he had taken the trouble of coming all that way, he should content himself with scanning the sea beside Gus.

What did the poor fool see? Gus could answer that already. "You see the sky, you've noted the black spots, you realize they are birds, like specks of dust, and you see the eddy of the ocean, what you would call waves, and that is that."

"Not so. Just like you, when I'm melancholic, I see the end of every living thing around me."

But Gus was not, in truth, melancholic. He was alert, lucid. If Buchanan had seen what he had, he would be overwhelmed by it, and would want to live like Gus, alone somewhere without any others like him. Gus looked out at the ocean, the immense flat expanse from which the whales had been drawn up under skies emptied of terns. For hours he had daydreamed, strangely, of a sterile leopard—one alone, of course—dragging out its existence on an African plain. The sounds around Gus were just a blur of noise to him, since the notes of the joyful great auk were missing from its harmony. He watched a blueprint of the universe roll out before him, the failed sketch of a new order devoid of new life, where the oddest forms, the rarest or most beautiful—an artichoke, a panther, a bat, a mandrake—were beginning to be erased, as though each year a new colour were lost.

Just then, Buchanan spoke. He uttered a short sentence, and Gus thought he could hear a ribbon inside it, silken and singing of an unfathomable gust of wind. He was returning to the beach of who knows which country, where Prosp lay dying, since old auks die, too, and being the last does not make you immortal. That is what he wanted to tell Prosp: that in the end, Prosp had lived the life of a great auk. And there on the beach Gus crawled over to the auk who lay in the seafoam, swirling the sand with his wings as a turtle does with its feet when returned to the ocean.

"Prosp," he said, "Don't be afraid, friend. Remember how light your feathers are, how strong you dove, how you caught fish, and the time you escaped the mouth of a whale with a sharp turn, or when you swam with another auk in the ocean current, a current like a corridor opening onto others, which you followed to the end. Remember how in the water a membrane closes over your eye, how your palate turns yellow in summer as you call to a mate, who also opens her beak, and how white spots form on both your faces for a time. Remember the two of you finding each other every summer, the love you felt for her, same as the love I felt for you, and the attachment you felt to me.

"Gus, you're smiling."

And this time Gus, who was smiling because he was talking to Prosp and everything had turned beautiful and simple once again, understood Buchanan's words as he spoke with a voice that no longer sounded like the wind whistling.

"Come back with me. Prosp can't be alive. He would be too old, eighteen years or thereabouts. No great auk has ever lived that long."

Gus already knew this, that Prosp was dead, because he was on the beach with Prosp, comforting him as he would have done if the auk were right here next to him. In truth, Gus was the one alone and Gus was the last—the last to have seen Prosp, this extraordinary race of marine cow, oviparous seal, an anomaly more stunning than a platypus, and the only bird-fish of that hemisphere.

Gus did not know why he was so obstinate to Buchanan's request, but he stood up. He still had something left to say.

"Look," he said, the word taking much effort to come out, "look, there's nothing left." Gus was pointing out into the distance. What he had meant to say was, "All the great auks are gone," but then he added, as though emphatic, "There are nothing but dead animals, and us—and we are near dead too."

He stopped short, his disdain for Buchanan preventing him from finishing. Despite these feelings, he kept walking next to him, because he knew Buchanan meant him well, that he loved Gus in his own way. Gus felt a warmth surround him, the reassuring sensation of the pity inspired in others, mixed with disdain on knowing Buchanan had not understood. If the earth had been flat, Gus would have said it was leaning just then on its side, like a plate, its contents sliding into an abyss. Yet the Scotsman continued to put one foot in front of the other as if everything were normal. He spoke to Gus as though he were a cherished pet, a loyal dog one whistles to so it will catch up. Prosp had not been a pet but a companion. Gus had never been a master, only a friend. He kept walking behind Buchanan, and stepped into the rowboat with him.

If it made Buchanan happy to think Gus was submitting, he saw no reason to correct him, really. The plate kept tilting, now near vertical as a gong, at its maximum rotation. In the rowboat sat Buchanan and the sailors, rowing, and Gus drifting into oblivion with Prosp and a stray baobab tree. Prosp was suddenly running under Elinborg's skirts, becoming tangled in them, Elinborg whom Gus had not seen arrive, and was entwined in Augustine's hair, as Ottarr, tugging on his sister's coat, held on to the auk's neck, and a ways away Mrs. Bridge appeared upside down, skirt around her shoulders and hat tilted on its side. Gus's scarf was about to blow away, and at first he tried to catch it, then gave up as he watched it drift through the baobab tree to land on a cathedral just emerged.

Far in the distance, Prosp waddled, released from Ottarr's grasp, as his feet paddled through the nothingness as though it were sand, his body teetering far to the left and then to the right, as always. Gus reached out, calling Prosp, but the auk did not hear. Then everyone tumbled—the great auk wobbly, head bobbing, the others at full speed—as though they had wings, though what good would wings have been? It was a steep fall, a fall into nothingness, a fall, Gus thought, into a world after Prosp.

And as Buchanan held his arm, Gus stepped onto the boat.

Author's Note

No historical tales of friendship between a person and a great auk have reached us. I was, however, able to refer to the ample documentation that exists on the species—officially extinct in 1844—to imagine the story of Gus and Prosp. We've known of the great auk's existence for at least 20,000 years, even if it is clearly much older. This is thanks to works of parietal art found in the Cosquer Cave near Marseille, France, that portray three auks, physically similar to the northern hemisphere penguin—not to be confused, of course, with the penguins of the southern hemisphere, even if the great auk, at eighty centimetres high, was nearly the size of a king penguin.

I would like to mention several books, without which I wouldn't have been able to write my own. Firstly, *Le Grand Pingouin*[1] by Henri Gourdin (Actes Sud, 2008), which was the first I read on the subject and one that I never stopped returning to. I cannot more highly recommend Henri Gourdin's biography of the nineteenth-century naturalist Jean-Jacques Audubon, which I sometimes evoked in these pages, *Du temps où les pingouins étaient nombreux...*[2] published in spring 2022 by Le Pommier, as I was rereading the manuscript before it went to print. But also Jean-Luc Porquet's *Lettre au dernier grand pingouin*[3] (Verticales, 2016), a meditation on the loss of experience a species' extinction always implies.

In Jeremy Gaskell's *Who Killed the Great Auk?* (Oxford University Press, 2001), I learned of William Proctor, a man who believed that the great auk went extinct in 1837. Despite his mistake, I loaned his experiences to Gus: that of discover-

1. [The Great Auk]
2. [From a Time When Penguins Were Many]
3. [Last Letter to a Great Auk]

ing a reality before being able to understand it, because your own era's ideas, theories, and ways of looking at things do not allow for it. Yet Proctor, and so Gus, intuited a reality we have lived in ever since, at a time when most experts believe a sixth mass extinction of species may be upon us.

To fully measure how difficult it was for a man in the years 1835 to 1850 to fathom the concept of extinction, a fundamental text is Julien Delord's *L'Extinction d'espèce. Histoire d'un concept & enjeux éthiques*[4] (Publications scientifiques du Muséum, 2010). Darwin only returned from his voyage on the Beagle after Gus had been to Eldey, and *On the Origin of Species* was only published in 1859. For people of Gus's time, the idea of evolution was not part of their thinking; the history of the world looked nothing like the evidence-based beliefs of today. The concept that a species could go extinct remained confined to paleontology, where it had become widespread since the discovery of mammoth bones in the late eighteenth century.

The dodo, which became emblematic of extinction, is the specimen that welcomes us into the extinct species hall of the Muséum national d'Histoire naturelle de Paris, where a stuffed great auk is conserved—rose to renown in 1848, near the end of Gus's adventure, thanks to the ornithologist Hugh Edwin Strickland and his book *The Dodo and Its Kindred*. Yet it was not until Lewis Carroll's *Alice in Wonderland* was published in 1865, where, as we know, the dodo plays a major role, that the dodo became world famous. On this bird, you can find William Broderip's article "The Dodo" published in *The Literary Gazette and Journal of Belles Lettres, Sciences and Arts* in 1852 as well as the much more recent one by Anthony S. Cheke and Samuel T. Turvey titled "Dead as a Dodo: The

4. [Species Extinction: History of a Concept and Ethical Implications]

Fortuitous Rise to Fame of an Extinction Icon" (*Historical Biology*, vol. 20, no. 2, 2008), and the book *Return of the Crazy Bird: The Sad, Strange Tale of the Dodo* by Clara Pinto-Correia (Copernicus Books, 2003).

To imagine the Faroe Islands at the time when Gus travelled there, I was inspired by the fascinating article that writer and translator Xavier Marmier published in *La Revue des deux mondes* in 1839. It is in this text, among others, that I discovered the profound and no doubt hypnotic songs of the Faroeans. I also owe much, for the scene on the portraits of young Augustine and Ottarr to an exhibition at Petit Palais in Paris from 2020 to 2021, "L'Âge d'or de la peinture danoise"[5], and the accompanying catalogue published by Paris Musées.

The list of books on animal behaviour, emotions, and thinking that I used as research is too long for this short note. But I must absolutely mention the work of Carl Safina, in particular his book *Qu'est-ce qui fait sourire les animaux?*[6] (Vuibert, 2018); and the work of sociologist Dominique Guillo, *Des chiens et des humains*[7] (Le Pommier, 2009), and *Les Fondements oubliés de la culture*[8] (Seuil, 2019), which, through the idea of "mutual adjustment of differences," offers fertile ground for describing what happens between humans and animals.

Finally, this novel would undoubtedly not exist had I not had the pleasure of editing the French edition of renowned ornithologist Joanna Burger's book *The Parrot Who Owns Me: The Story of a Relationship* for Plein Jour, (originally published in English by Villard, 2001). Many thanks to her and her friend Tiko.

5. [The Golden Age of Danish Painting]
6. [What Makes Animals Smile?]
7. [Dogs and Humans]
8. [The Forgotten Foundations of Culture]

Translator's Note

In addition to the works cited by the author, in translating Grimbert's book, I referred often to Gísli Pálsson's recent and comprehensive text on the history of the great auk, whose title was no doubt inspired by Grimbert's French novel (*The Last of Its Kind: The Search for the Great Auk and the Discovery of Extinction*, Princeton University Press, 2024). I owe a great debt to *Golden Bird: Two Orkney Stories* by George Mackay Brown (many thanks to the Orcadian bookshop for this recommendation), which provided the feel of the Orkneys in the English language during Gus's era; and to Cosmo Sheldrake's 2020 album *Wake Up Calls* comprised of the sounds of endangered birds, which accompanied my translation throughout. And many thanks to the penguins at the Montréal Biodôme, whom I sometimes visited and sketched, imagining the way they preened themselves and gulped down fish to be somewhat similar to the behaviours of the great auk.

About the Author

SIBYLLE GRIMBERT's eleventh novel, *Le dernier des siens* (2022) was a finalist for the Femina, Renaudot, Femina Lycéens, and Renaudot Lycéens prizes, and the Grand Prix de l'Académie française. The book has been translated into many languages, including English as *The Last of Its Kind* (tr. by Aleshia Jensen), and an animated film is forthcoming. Grimbert is also a recipient of the prestigious Maurice Genevoix Prize from the Académie Française, the 30 Millions D'Amis Literary Prize, the François Sommer Prize, and the Joseph Kessel Prize. She lives in Paris.

PHOTO: TIFFANY MEYER

About the Translator

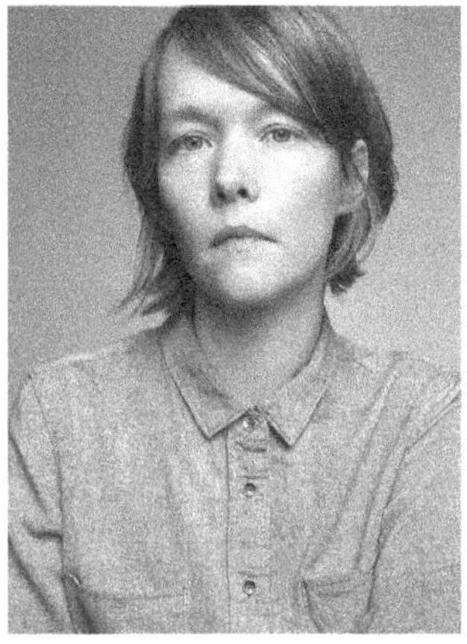

ALESHIA JENSEN is a literary translator and former bookseller living in Tio'tia:ke / Montréal. A four-time finalist for the Governor General's Literary Award for Translation, Jensen translates Quebec and French fiction and indie comics. Her translations include *Remnants* by Céline Huyghebaert, *Prague* by Maude Veilleux, in co-translation with Aimee Wall, as well as graphic novels by Mirion Malle, María Medem, and Camille Jourdy.

PHOTO: JUSTINE LATOUR

Colophon

Manufactured as the first English edition of
The Last of Its Kind
in the fall of 2025 by Book*hug Press

Edited for the press by Pablo Strauss
Copy edited by Laurie Siblock
Proofread by Susan Sanford Blades
Type + design by Malcolm Sutton
Cover Image: 'Great Auk' by John Duncan / public domain

Printed in Canada

bookhugpress.ca